GW00776798

Blood Sport

A.J. Carella

PUBLISHED BY:
A.J. Carella

Enfield Libraries

91200000340632

Copyright © 2014

www.facebook.com/ajcarella
www.twitter.com/@ajcarella

All rights reserved.

No part of this publication may be copied, reproduced in any format, by any means, electronic or otherwise, without prior consent from the copyright owner and publisher of this book.

This is a work of fiction. All characters, names, places and events are the product of the author's imagination or used fictitiously.

One

It looked like a pile of rags by the side of the road and she would have driven past were it not for a slight movement that caught her eye as she drew alongside. It was getting dark. It was the end of a long day and she thought maybe her eyes were playing tricks on her. *Best check it out,* Kat told herself as she stopped the car, put it in reverse and backed up.

There wasn't much along this road, being several miles out from Brecon Point. She was only on it as the storm that had been raging most of the day had brought down a tree across the road she would normally have taken home. Unfortunately, around here if a road was blocked and unless you were prepared to drive across fields, you usually had to travel several miles out of your way to get to where you wanted to go.

As she pulled the car alongside and stopped, the pile moved again. *Don't be an idiot, Kat,* she told herself. *You're on an empty road, after dark with no one around for miles.* Although she had a permit to carry a firearm, she rarely did these days but she did carry pepper spray, which she now got out of her purse and gripped tightly in her hand before opening the car door.

She was getting a bad feeling as she drew closer to the pile and it started to take shape. That feeling turned to shock as the reality of what she was looking at hit her like a punch to the gut. He was so filthy that at first it had been hard to see where his dirty clothes ended and his torn and bloodied skin began, but now there was no mistaking that she was looking at a severely beaten human being.

Having been a police officer for many years for the LAPD, she had seen more than her fair share of beaten and broken bodies, usually on a Friday or Saturday night outside various bars. But this was different. Much different. This victim couldn't have been much older than twelve years old.

He was lying on his back with his eyes closed. Dropping to her knees in the dirt next to him, Kat reached out and gently touched his cheek. At the touch, the boy's eyes flickered open and he looked straight at her. The desperation and fear she saw in them took her breath away. "You're safe now. I'm going to get help." The boy just closed his eyes again with a sigh.

Shit! The nearest hospital was in the next town and she knew that if she called for an ambulance, it would take forever to get there. From the condition he was in, she didn't know how much time the boy had and if she could afford to wait that long.

Brecon point was a small town but it was much closer and there was a town doctor. Decision made, Kat stood up, went to her car and opened the back door. Returning to the boy, she gently lifted him into her arms. He was much lighter than she'd expected and she could feel through his rags that he was nothing but skin and bone. Gently carrying him to her car, she laid him on the back seat. He moaned slightly as she did, but he didn't open his eyes again.

Getting into the driver's seat, she grabbed her phone from her purse and quickly called the police station in town and told them what she'd found. As it was after hours the doctor's office would be closed, but they assured her that they would make sure the doctor would be there waiting for her.

Two

Kat stood in a corner of the room, not wanting to get in the way, as Dr. Crichton examined the child. She watched her as she carefully peeled away his dirty and torn clothes to look for injuries. Kat couldn't help but flinch as every wound was revealed.

When she'd arrived at the clinic the light had been on and the doctor had been there waiting for them. Taking one look at the child cradled in Kat's arms, she had ushered them into an examination room before immediately telling Kat to call an ambulance.

"Where did you find him?" She jumped at the sound of the voice behind her. She hadn't heard him come in. Chief Finlay had been chief when she'd first left town twenty years ago and now, pushing sixty-five, he showed no sign of slowing down.

"Hi, Chief," she said, acknowledging his arrival. "I found him by the side of the road on the way back from work." She shook her head. "If he hadn't moved, I would have driven right past him."

"It's a good thing you didn't." It was Doctor Crichton who spoke, drawing their attention. "This poor kid has suffered a severe beating. He has a broken arm, a concussion and severe lacerations all over his body. I'll need to get him to the hospital immediately to make sure there's nothing more serious going on internally. If he'd been there all night, there's no knowing if he would have survived."

"I'll go with you," Kat said immediately. She didn't want to leave this poor boy's side.

"Sorry, Kat, but we'll take it from here." The chief put his hand on her shoulder gently. "It's a police matter now."

Kat opened her mouth to argue but then closed it again. She knew he was right. She wasn't a police officer anymore. This had nothing to do with her, but the thought of leaving him all alone was killing her. But she had no choice. Though he probably couldn't hear her, she wanted to say goodbye, to tell him it was going to be okay, so she walked over to him. Leaning down, she whispered in his ear, "it's okay, you're safe now." He moved slightly then, inching his hand over to grip hers where it rested on the side of the examination table. She tried to gently pull it away, but he gripped it harder still. With tears in her eyes, she looked at the chief. "I can't leave him."

"If she makes him feel safer, she should stay with him. We don't know the full extent of his injuries yet and we should avoid doing anything that's likely to upset him," Dr. Crichton said, addressing the chief.

Kat held her breath while he considered this and, after a brief pause, he nodded brusquely. "Okay, the doc's right. Our main priority has to be making sure this little guy is okay. You can go with him. But Kat," he carried on as she turned back to the boy, "he is a crime scene and I don't have to tell you that you are now, too. And if he says anything, anything at all, you let me know. Got it?" Kat nodded. "Of course, Chief. Thank you."

He nodded. "I'll get an officer and CSI to meet you at the hospital as soon as we've secured the area where he was found."

The flashing of blue and red lights through the clinic window told them that the ambulance had arrived. Kat watched as he was loaded onto a gurney and put in the back before climbing in next to him and taking his hand in hers.

"I'm here and I'm not going anywhere," she told him as the doors closed and they left for the hospital.

Three

He went over what they knew so far in his head as he made his way out to the main crime scene, which wasn't much. When the chief had called on the radio to tell him to get out there and secure the area where the kid had been found, he'd also told him that Kat had had the foresight to leave the warning triangle from her trunk by the side of the road so they'd be able to find the exact spot again. He was driving slowly so that he didn't miss it and sure enough, his lights hit the red plastic and it reflected back at him. Pulling over, he got out of his cruiser and shrugged on his coat. *CSI better hurry up,* he thought as he looked up at the sky. Storms had been battering the area all day and while it had been dry for the last few hours, it looked like it wouldn't stay that way for long.

The wind ruffled his hair as he stood with his hands in his coat pockets, leaning against the hood of the car. There was nothing he could do until CSI got there and he could have waited in the car, but he'd been sitting down most of the day and needed to stretch his legs.

He was suffering from conflicting emotions. Part of him wanted to call Kat and make sure she was okay. What she'd come across wasn't nice and would have upset even an experienced police officer but the other part, the part that he'd been listening to the for the past few months, warned him to stay away. Until she'd turned up looking for her niece all those months ago he'd thought he'd put the past behind him, but her reappearance had opened all those old wounds. While searching for her niece, though, he'd grown close to her again and all the feelings he'd once had for her had started to re-emerge.

When she'd finally told him what had made her leave, though, he'd been floored. He hadn't known how to react, still didn't, so he'd avoided her ever since, acknowledging her when he did see her about town but no more than that. He knew he was probably hurting her but he couldn't help it. He needed to figure out how to deal with what she'd told him.

Lights in the distance snapped him out of his reverie and told him that the crime scene techs had arrived. Kat was tough. She didn't need him to hold her hand and he had a job to do.

A flash of lightning lit up the sky, then was closely followed by a loud clap of thunder. As he'd feared, big fat drops of rain started to fall slowly at first, gathering momentum until they were coming down fast and heavy.

"Come on, quickly!" he urged the techs as they climbed out of their vehicle. "We need to get a canopy up now!" Helping them pull it out of the back of their truck, they worked as quickly as they could, getting it up in less than two minutes. Finn's heart sank, though, as he looked at the ground. It was already a soggy mess and it was likely that any trace evidence that had been there had been washed away.

"Do what you can, guys." He sighed, climbing back into the dry interior of his cruiser. He knew that he was going to be here a while, so he rested his head back against the headrest and closed his eyes. He had a feeling it was going to be a long night.

Four

The room had that typical hospital smell but was different in most other ways. After being thoroughly examined and the doctors having found no further injuries, he had been transferred to this single room on the children's ward. The walls were painted a bright sunny yellow and were covered in stickers of SpongeBob and superheroes and various other figures that Kat didn't recognize. Brightly-colored curtains hung on the windows and there was a box of stuffed toys and children's books set in the corner. It seemed in sharp contrast to the young boy who laid on the bed. He seemed too small for it and his tiny frame looked lost in the bright white sheets. The cuts and bruises on his body were even more apparent now than when he'd first been found. Though the nurses had tried to remove as much of the blood as they could, without a proper bath much of it remained and it added to the illusion that surely he must be in the wrong place.

After settling him in to his room, Dr. Crichton had gone to talk to the hospital doctors about his condition as he was now her patient, leaving Kat by the side of his bed holding his hand. He still hadn't regained full consciousness but every now and then she felt a squeeze on her hand, as if he was checking she was still there, and she made sure she squeezed back to reassure him.

She'd called Jamie shortly after they'd arrived at the hospital to let her know where she was and why. She didn't want her to worry when she didn't come home. She smiled to herself as she thought of Jamie. She'd come a long way since she'd disappeared a couple of years ago, attacked by her brother's girlfriend and left for dead. She'd lost her memory as a result and it had been a year-and-a-half before she'd been found and brought home. Unfortunately, it had not been before her parents were killed in a car wreck. Her brother, Jake, was in prison and Jamie would have been all alone had Kat not decided to accept her offer of a job in the family firm to come back to Brecon Point and live with her. Kat had been unsure at first. Giving up her job with the LAPD had been a big step but she'd felt she needed to make up for not having been around when her family needed her.

But she'd been pleasantly surprised. Yes, there was no doubt she missed her job, the adrenaline rush when she was on a case and the satisfaction of putting criminals behind bars, but she was also enjoying her new job and she was loving being with her niece. She hadn't realized just how much she'd missed being part of a family until now.

A squeeze on her hand brought her attention back to the small body lying in the bed. *Who could do such a thing?* It was difficult to judge his age, he was small and clearly undernourished. His skin was also very pale. A pale that came not from just being unwell, but the more profound pale that you get when you haven't been outdoors for a long time. It broke her heart to see him lying there and she hoped he had a family somewhere that cared for him and were missing him.

As she looked at him, his eyelids started to flutter before opening properly for the first time since she'd found him, revealing green eyes that were filled with sadness as they looked at her. "Hey, how are you feeling?" She kept her voice low as she stood up and leaned in to him, not wanting to scare him.

He didn't reply; he just looked at her, unblinking. "I bet you'd like a drink?" she asked him, not expecting an answer. She filled a plastic tumbler from a jug on the side table and held it to his lips while he lifted his head to take a sip. He never took his eyes off her and tracked her movements as she put the glass down when he finished.

"My name is Kat and I'm the one who found you." His shallow breathing and the way his hands gripped the bed sheets told her he was scared and she hoped that by talking to him it may help him to relax. "You're safe now, I promise you." She smiled at him before sitting down again, pulling her chair closer to the bed and taking his hand in hers again.

As well as the window to the outside, there was a window in the wall separating the room from the corridor to allow the nursing staff to keep an eye on their patient. Through it, she saw that Finn had arrived and was talking to Dr. Crichton in the corridor just outside. "Honey, I need to just pop outside for a minute, okay?" she told the kid gently and tried to pull her hand away from his but he wouldn't let go, shaking his head vehemently with tears filling his eyes. "It's okay. I promise I'll be right back and I'll just be right outside the door, okay?" This time he let her remove her hand, but he kept his eyes firmly glued to her as she stood and left the room.

She saw Finn tense and stand a little straighter as she walked towards where they were talking in low voices, but he didn't turn and acknowledge her. They had barely spoken in the last six months and she had no idea what was going on in his head, but right now they both needed to put their differences aside. "Dr. Crichton, Finn, he's just woken up," she told them when she got close.

"It's Sally, please" the woman replied. "I was just telling Finn about his medical status. As you know, thankfully, there were no internal injuries. However, the x-rays did reveal multiple old bone fractures that have either healed or are partially healed." She sighed. "This poor kid has been regularly beaten over a long period of time." She put her hand on Finn's arm. "I'll go and check on him. I'll catch up with you a bit later." And, with a smile to Kat, she turned and walked off.

Kat watched her leave. She'd called him Finn, not Officer Groves and the hand on the arm told of a certain familiarity. The knowledge threw her for a moment; she hadn't been aware that he was involved with anyone. She'd heard that he'd split from his last girlfriend around the time they'd brought Jamie home and, naively perhaps, she'd assumed he was still single. She couldn't pretend the knowledge didn't hurt. It did, but she had no claim on him.

"I'll need to speak to him, then, if he's awake."

"Sorry?" With a start, she realized Finn was looking at her and had just spoken.

"I said that I'll need to speak to him," he said with that knowing look on his face, the one that said he knew exactly what she was thinking. "Has he said anything?"

"No, not a word." She refocused on the matter at hand. "Be gentle with him. He's terrified."

"Of course I'll be gentle. I have done this before, you know." He frowned.

"I'm sorry, I didn't mean that the way it came out." She turned and glanced through the window at where the boy lay. "I'm just feeling a bit protective."

He nodded. "Exactly why you need to go now before you get any more attached." He held up his hand as she was about to speak, cutting her off. "Kat, the chief let you come with him to the hospital but he's here now. He's safe. It's time for you to leave us to do our job." More gently, he told her, "I know it's hard, but you can't let yourself get too attached."

"I can't go, Finn. I promised him I wouldn't leave him."

"For God's sake, Kat, you know better than that!"

He was right, she did know better than that. But this boy had wrapped himself around her heart and wasn't about to let go and she wasn't about to break her promise, either.

"Look, why don't you let me stay until you find his family at least?" she asked. "What harm can it do?"

Finn sighed. "I'll have to check with the chief, Kat. It's not my decision and I'm not making any promises." He turned toward the boy's room. "Right now, though, I need to talk to him and you need to stay out here. Can you do that, do you think?"

Kat ignored his sarcasm and nodded. "Of course. I'll go and get a coffee."

He didn't reply, turning and striding towards the boy's room just as Dr. Crichton was coming out. Kat had just turned away when she heard the screeching. It sounded like a cornered animal screaming for its life and it was coming from the boy's room. Running back as fast as she could, she flung open the door to find the boy huddled on the floor in a corner, his arms crossed over his head, screaming. Finn was standing at the other side of the room looking startled and he looked at Kat as she walked in, pleading with his eyes for her to do something.

"It's okay. I'm here, and no one is going to hurt you," she said in a low voice crouching down beside the boy and looking over at Finn, indicating with her head that he needed to leave the room.

Nodding, he seemed relieved as he turned and walked out leaving her to try and calm the boy down. As soon as Finn left, the screaming stopped and he was calming down, his breathing returning to normal. Gently helping him to his feet, she got him back into bed before sitting on the edge and holding his hand.

"That man, the one that was just in here, he's a friend of mine," she told him. "He's a really good man, a policeman, who wants to help you. His name is Finn." She had an idea that she knew why he'd reacted so strongly. "Was it a man who hurt you?" He confirmed her fears when he nodded. "Okay, well this man, Finn, would never hurt you. Do you think we could ask him to come back in?"

The boy started to cry then, shaking his head. "How about if I stay with you? Would it be okay then?" He looked her in the eyes and she hoped that he knew he could trust her. He nodded. "Okay, I'll just go and tell him. Thank you for being so brave."

Joining Finn outside the room where he was waiting, she told him what had just happened. "I know it's not ideal but he wants me there when you talk to him. He's terrified of men, Finn, and he seems to have taken a shine to me." She jutted out her chin. "And I won't leave him." She was waiting for him to make another argument but he surprised her.

"Agreed." His face was somber. "I called the chief while you were in there and he's okayed it. With your background, you won't mess it up and we need him to talk to us. Apart from anything else, the poor guy needs to have someone around him that he feels safe with and it looks like that someone is you."

Five

If he ever found whoever had done this to the poor kid, he wasn't sure he'd be able to stop himself from beating him to a pulp. He'd sat in the bed clutching Kat's hand like his life depended on it, and even though he'd been standing on the other side of the room he'd flinched every time Finn spoke. He'd put his questions to him gently, hoping that he would be able to give them something, anything, that would help them, but he'd gotten nothing. In fact, the boy hadn't spoken at all, merely nodding or shaking his head in answer. He hadn't even been able to tell them his name, just shaking his head when he'd asked.

Not wanting to push him too hard, he'd left Kat with him and had headed back to the station. He was hoping that CSI might have something to give him. They'd taken the kid's DNA at the hospital and he was hoping that it was in a database somewhere. There was a chance, a very slim one, that if the kid had been reported missing the local PD would have taken a sample of DNA from his home and entered it in the system.

"How's the boy?" the chief asked, coming to stand by his desk.

Finn shook his head. "Not good. The doc says there's no medical reason for it but he won't talk. I've left Kat with him. He seems to really trust her so maybe she can get somewhere." He frowned at the thought of Kat. That woman had a way of getting under his skin; there was no denying it. He'd watched as she'd sat on the boy's bed talking to him in a low soothing voice and had been struck by what a natural she was with him. Rather than make his feelings towards her soften, though, it had just left him even more confused.

"So we still have no idea who he is?"

"No, none. I'm hoping that we might get something from the lab." The phone on his desk interrupted them and Finn grabbed, it hoping it was the results he was waiting for. He listened for a minute, writing notes as the chief looked on. Finally, he put the phone down with a smile and held up the paper he'd been writing on.

"We've got a DNA hit!" He could barely believe they'd gotten so lucky. "The kid is Daniel Lytchett, age twelve." His fingers started flying on his computer keyboard as he spoke to the chief, inputting the information to find out more. "He was reported missing six years ago from Torino by his parents." He paused as he read more. "He was on his way home from school. He got off the school bus to walk the short distance from there to his house, but he never arrived."

That must be a parent's worst nightmare, he thought "There's a number here for the officer dealing with the case. I'll give him a call."

"Torino? That's got to be what, five hundred miles from here? How on earth did a kid who went missing that far away end up here?" The chief shook his head. "No matter. At least we'll be able to make one family incredibly happy today." He checked his watch. "I'm going to check in with the others. They're checking the area where the kid was found, but at this time of night I don't think they'll find much."

As soon as the chief had gone, Finn picked up the phone and dialed the number listed on the file. "Officer Pelks?" Finn spoke as the phone at the other end was picked up.

"Yes, can I help you?"

"I'm Officer Groves, calling from Brecon Point PD. I'm calling about a case you dealt with a few years ago, a missing boy by the name of Daniel Lytchett."

"Went missing on his way home from school. I remember it." There was a pause on the end of the phone. "It was one of those cases, you know? One of the ones that you don't forget."

"Well, we had a bit of an incident here last night and it looks like we might have found him."

"Found his body, you mean?"

Finn smiled, enjoying this part of his job. "No, I mean we found him alive."

There was a sharp intake of breath on the other end of the phone "I don't believe it. I was sure that we were only ever going to find his remains. Dear God, if only it had been six months sooner."

Finn was confused but officer Pelks went on to explain, and what he told him made his blood run cold.

***

Finn sat in silence at his desk, taking in what he had just heard. Despite years of investigating and never giving up hope, Officer Pelks and the boy's family had never been able to come up with any leads at all and the case had gone completely cold. The Lytchett's had remained in the same home where they'd been living when Daniel went missing, and it was on a drive back to this house after attending a fundraiser for missing children just six months ago that the accident had happened. A trailer had skidded on black ice and jacknifed before toppling over and crushing the Lytchett's car. They didn't survive. They died without ever knowing what had happened to their son. Unexpectedly, this thought brought tears to Finn's eyes and he brushed them away with the back of his hand. *Dammit!* According to Officer Pelks, the kid had no other family, so he was all alone in the world now. *Hasn't he gone through enough?* he thought angrily.

Checking the clock on the wall, he realized it was now past midnight and his shift had ended hours ago. Long hours were part of the job, though, and he still had a lot to do before he could go home. Pushing his chair away from his desk, he stood up and walked over to the chief's office. The door was open, but Finn knocked on the glass anyway before walking in and filling him in on the conversation he'd just had.

The chief shook his head. "As if the poor kid doesn't have enough to deal with," he said wryly. "This needs to be handled sensitively. Get together with Dr. Crichton about the best way to move forward. We don't want to do anything that's likely to get in the way of his recovery. We'll also need to contact Child Protective Services as he has no legal guardian."

Finn nodded. "Okay, I'll speak to Dr. Crichton as soon as I can. She was still at the hospital when I left. I'll contact CPS in the morning. He's going to have to stay in the hospital overnight anyway and he's safe and settled where he is for now. "

The chief nodded. "Okay. CSI are still at the original scene but there's nothing more you can do tonight. After you've spoken to the doc, go home and get some rest."

"Will do." He turned to leave. "Night, Chief."

Six

He'd planned on going home and calling Sally, but halfway there he'd turned the car around and headed to the hospital instead. He tried to convince himself it was because he wanted to see Sally, but he knew that the real reason was one he didn't want to admit to himself. He wanted to see Kat, wanted to make sure she was okay. *Why did she get to him so much?* He'd dated many women, married one, but none had had the effect on him that Kat did. When he didn't see her he managed to push thoughts of her to one side, almost pretending she didn't exist; but when he found himself in her orbit, she was all he could think about. Even now, when he was dating someone else and should be thinking about her, thoughts of Kat were in the place where thoughts of her should be.

As he turned the cruiser into the hospital parking lot he made himself a promise. After this case was over he would sit down with Kat and sort this out once and for all. But to do that he needed to sort out his own feelings and he wasn't there yet. Admittedly, to do that he needed to actually sit down and think about it, which was something he had been studiously avoiding. He couldn't avoid it forever, though.

Seven

She'd fallen asleep with her head resting on the bed, his small hand still clutched in hers. The curtains were drawn now and the room was dark except for the gentle glow under the door given off by the lights in the hall outside. It had taken him a long time to settle at first, and the first time he'd fallen asleep it had only been a few minutes before he'd woken screaming, gripped in the throes of a terrible nightmare. Kat had sat and cuddled him, reassuring him gently until he'd finally managed to go back to sleep. Now the sound of his gentle breathing was the only sound in the room and it was like a balm to her heart. Gently pulling her hand from his without waking him, she stood up and stretched. *God, I need a coffee.* She turned to the door, intending to go and grab one from the machine down the hall.

"Don't leave me." The words were barely more than a whisper, but the plea behind them was deafening. She quickly went back to the bed and took his hand in hers. "So you can speak!" She smiled gently at him. "Don't worry, I'm not leaving you. I was just going to grab a drink. Is that okay?"

"Okay." he whispered.

"Would you like some candy from the machine? Don't tell the nurses. It'll be our little secret." She winked.

A small flutter of a smile crossed his lips and he nodded.

"Okay, I'll be right back." She squeezed his hand and left the room, closing the door gently behind her.

***

"Damn machine!" she cursed under her breath. It had taken her money but wouldn't give her the candy. There was no way she was going back empty-handed. It might only be a candy bar, but she had a feeling this kid had been let down enough and she wasn't about to do it to him again.

"Need help?"

She hadn't heard him come up behind her. "Hi, Finn. Yes, please. This damn machine won't work." She watched as he put his hands on the top of the machine and gently rocked it back and forth until, with a satisfying clunk, the candy dropped into the tray at the bottom. "Neat trick," she said, reaching in for it. "You must have done that before."

He laughed. "Yes, we have history, this machine and I." His face turned serious. "How's the kid doing?"

"Well, he spoke to me, so that's a good sign. But after what he went through, I'd be lying if I said he's okay." She turned and started walking back to the room and Finn fell into step beside her. "Have you managed to find out who he is yet?"

Finn nodded. "Yes. His name is Daniel. He went missing six years ago."

"Six years? Where on earth has he been all that time?"

"That's what we need to find out."

"Poor kid. Any news on his family?"

Finn pulled up short. "Unfortunately, yes." He filled her in on what he'd found out so far.

"Oh my God. That's awful!" She'd assumed there was a family out there looking for him and the news that he was all alone broke her heart. "What's going to happen to him now?"

Finn shrugged. "We don't have any choice. We're going to have to contact CPS." He didn't look happy at the thought. "They'll find him foster parents for now."

Kat shook her head. "No."

"What do you mean, no? Kat, we have no choice."

She didn't know what made her blurt it out but she just knew there was no way she was letting this kid go into foster care. "No. He's going to come home with me."

Finn looked taken aback. "Really? You'd do that?"

"Absolutely." She knew without a shadow of a doubt that it was the right thing to do. "This kid has been through so much, more than we probably even realize. He seems to trust me. It makes sense that he come home with me. For now at least."

"Okay. Well, I'll have to clear it with CPS, make sure they're okay with it, but I'm sure it will be fine." He gave her a hard look. "Are you sure you want to do this? It won't be a walk in the park, you know. He's bound to have problems after this."

"What? And you think because a kid might have problems they don't deserve a good home?" She could feel herself getting angry.

"No, that's not what I meant at all and you know it. I meant it's going to be hard and with everything that happened with Jamie and Jake I just want you to think about it, be sure you're up to it."

"I'm sure." She stuck her chin out defiantly.

"Okay. Well I'll call them in the morning and make the arrangements then."

"Thanks, Finn." She stopped walking as they arrived outside the room. "You'd better not come in. He seems calmer and I'd hate for him to get upset again."

Finn immediately agreed "Of course. I came to see Sally anyway so I'd better go and track her down."

Kat hated the feeling those words gave her, but that was her problem not his. "Could you tell her that he's spoken to me? It'll save me having to go and find her."

"No problem." He opened the door to the room for her. "I'll catch up with you tomorrow. Try and get some rest."

"I will. Thank you, Finn."

Eight

After their midnight snack, she'd curled up in the chair beside Daniel's bed and tried to get some sleep herself. It wasn't easy; the chair was not designed to encourage long stays and she'd kept waking up when she lost the feeling in various parts of her body. She'd finally given up at five a.m. and she was very conscious of how awful she must look when Dr. Crichton arrived shortly after they'd served breakfast. It was hard not to be. Despite having been at the hospital until late the night before, there was no sign of tiredness on Sally's face, her skin looking fresh and flawless. She was very petite, only about 5' 2" and very slim. Her blonde hair was cut in a pixie style which showed off her high cheekbones to their full advantage. Her easy glamor was making Kat feel like an ugly duckling but she had to grudgingly concede that Finn had good taste in women. That thought didn't make her feel any happier about it, though.

Kat stood back as she examined him. "That's great, Daniel, thank you. I'm just going to have a quick word with Kat outside." At her prompting, Kat stood and followed her out of the room.

"I'm pleased to say that he's well enough to be released. Physically, he will mend; what damage has been done psychologically, though, it's too early to say." She handed Kat a large brown envelope filled with papers. "We've had a call from CPS allowing us to release him into your care."

"That's wonderful news. Thank you. What's all this?"

"They've arranged for him to see a psychologist and all the details are in there. There are also some forms in there that we need you sign before you leave. You can drop them at the desk when you go."

"Okay, no problem." She was just about to turn and go back into the room when Sally stopped her.

"One more thing, Kat. Finn and I talked last night about how best to break the news to him about his family. We both agreed it would be best if it came from you. How do you feel about that?"

She'd be lying if she said she wanted to do it, but they were right; it would be best coming from her. "I think you're right. It's going to be heart-breaking for him and he seems to trust me more than anyone else, so it makes sense."

"Okay, great. I'll let Finn know."

Checking that Daniel could still see her through the window, she gave him a little wave before pulling her phone out of pocket to call Jamie.

"I was just about to call you," Jamie said when she answered. "How is he this morning?"

Kat filled her in on his condition and on what they'd learned about him since the night before.

"The poor kid! That's awful. What's going to happen to him now?"

"Well, that's just it. I should have checked with you first, I know, but I told Finn that he could come and stay with us for now. Is that okay with you?" Kat knew she should have asked before she'd said, it but she doubted very much that Jamie would have an issue with it.

"Of course he must. Absolutely," Jamie confirmed.

"That's great. Thanks, Jamie. Well, they've just given him the all clear to be taken home so do you think you could come and pick us up? I came in the ambulance last night and don't have my car here."

"No problem. I'll leave right now."

"Could you also go by the store and grab him some clothes? All his clothes were taken for evidence. Not that I'd want him to have to put them on again."

"Not a problem. I'll get there as soon as I can."

Kat disconnected the call and headed back to the boy's room. She was looking forward to getting him out of there; a hospital was no place for a kid. Besides, if she had to be the one to break the news about his parents, she didn't want to do it here. He hadn't asked about them, but from what Finn had told her, he had been gone so long his memory of them may well have faded. Still, it was not a conversation she was looking forward to and she wanted him to be in a place he felt safe when she told him.

"Okay, young man." she said, sitting on the edge of the bed. "My niece is on her way with some clothes for you to get changed into and then we can get out of this place. How does that sound?" The smile told her that that sounded very good to him.

"You're going to come home with me for now. Is that okay with you?" He nodded, the smile still on his face, and Kat felt her heart clench. "While we're waiting, why don't you go and take a shower and clean up?" He was still covered in the dried blood and dirt that the nurses hadn't been able to remove with a sponge and Kat wanted him to leave it all behind at the hospital along with the clothes he came in wearing. It was all part of his past; he needed to look to the future now.

"You won't go?"

"No, I won't go. I'll sit right here on the bed and wait for you and I'll be here when you're done."

He looked much better after he'd showered. It wasn't long after that that there was a knock on the door and Jamie popped her head around.

"Come in, there's someone I'd like you to meet." Kat waved her in. "Jamie, this is Daniel."

"Hi, Daniel. I'm very pleased to meet you."

Kat was pleased to see that he gave her a small smile.

"I've brought you some clothes." She put a plastic bag on the bed.

"Thanks, Jamie." Kat turned to Daniel. "Okay, we'll give you some privacy to get changed, okay?" She stood up from the bed and, with Jamie, left the room, turning to pull the door closed behind her. As she did, she caught a glimpse of him as he removed his hospital issued gown and her breath caught in her throat. His back was a criss cross of scars. Some newly healed, some that had obviously been there for a long time. The sight made her stomach heave and her jaw clench. *I'll find who did this to you and then the bastard will pay,* she promised him silently before closing the door.

Nine

He was surprised to find the full crime scene report sitting on his desk when he had arrived this morning. They usually had to wait much long for the lab to get back to them, but they'd obviously pulled out all the stops for this one. He'd finally gotten home from the hospital at two a.m. and it was now seven thirty a.m. He hadn't managed to sleep, but had made himself lie on his bed with his eyes closed trying to rest. He'd only managed that for about an hour before the images of the kid in his mind and the thoughts of what might have happened to him became too much; he had to get up. He'd spent the rest of the night in his garage working on the classic car he was lovingly restoring, allowing his thoughts to roam. Pushing thoughts of the case aside, he allowed himself to think about his personal life. He liked Sally. They hadn't been dating that long but she was smart, attractive and didn't come with the history he shared with Kat.

But it was exactly because of that history with Kat that he didn't seem to be able to shake the feeling that he should be with her, not Sally. The problem was that he didn't know if he could get past all the things she'd done, as much as he might want to. Finally giving up on coming to an answer, he packed his tools away at about five a.m. and went for a run. After a shower and change, he'd headed in to work.

***

He hadn't expected much but the report was still disappointing, revealing little. The rain that had fallen before they'd had chance to erect the shelter over the scene had washed away any trace evidence, if there had even been any. There were no footprints, no tire tracks, or anything else that could give them any kind of a lead. The boy himself had been examined as soon as the doctors had determined that his injuries were not life-threatening and the results of that examination were also included in the report.

Thankfully, this had yielded more. Scrapings had been taken from under his nails and his clothing had been examined for trace evidence. It made for confusing reading, though. According to the report, his dirty clothes were covered in the DNA of several other people in the form of blood, mainly, but also sweat and saliva. The scrapings had taken from under his nails had also revealed multiple DNA profiles. *Did that mean there were multiple offenders?*

The DNA profiles had been run through every database they had access to and they hadn't had a single match, which surprised him. He would have expected at least one of them to be known to them already.

Looking around, it suddenly dawned on him how quiet it was. Theirs was a very small police department with a grand total of six patrol officers, including him, and the chief. They had no dedicated specialist departments, so when a big case hit it usually ended up on his desk as the longest serving and experienced officer, second to the chief himself.

It suited him. Kat had asked him once why he didn't move to one of the big cities where promotion was more likely, but he had no desire to. Here, he was a patrol officer, a homicide detective, a narcotics detective and a lot more all rolled into one. But in all his years, he could count on one hand the number of times he'd arrived before the chief in the morning.

The vibrating of his cell in his pants pocket got his attention and, with a sigh, he saw that the caller was Sally. He'd been dating someone when Kat had re-appeared in town six months earlier, but he'd quickly realized he still had feelings for Kat. Even after her bombshell, he knew that he couldn't keep pretending so he'd ended it with the woman he'd been seeing.

He hadn't dated anyone since then until very recently. Sally had only arrived in town a few weeks ago and they'd met during a domestic violence case he'd been dealing with. The victim had refused to go to the hospital for her injuries but had agreed to be seen by a doctor at home. Calling the clinic, expecting to speak to old Doc James, he'd been surprised when he'd gotten her instead. She'd immediately agreed to come out to the old Jenkins farm and, despite the circumstances, they'd hit it off. As he'd walked her out to her car, he'd asked her out for dinner and she'd agreed. They'd been on a few dates since. He enjoyed her company, but he didn't know if he wanted to take it to the next level.

He was tempted to allow the call to go to voicemail, but realizing it could be important he picked up.

"Hi, Sally."

"Finn, where are you?"

The tone of her voice told him something was wrong. "I'm at the office. Why? What's wrong?"

"Finn, I'm sorry. You need to get over here as soon as you can. I'm at the hospital."

"Oh God, please don't tell me anything's happened to the kid." *Had he taken a turn for the worse? Did they miss something?* Immediately his thoughts turned to how Kat would take it. So much so that he wasn't prepared for what came next.

"No, Finn, Daniel is fine. It's the chief. He had a major heart attack this morning. His wife called an ambulance and he was brought straight here. He arrived about an hour ago."

He didn't hear the end of the sentence, having already disconnected, and he was out of the door before she even realized he wasn't listening any more.

***

He'd broken every speed limit on the way there and as he pushed through the door into the hospital, his heart was beating almost out of his chest. *This can't be happening!* The chief had been the one who had straightened him out when he was just a naive kid setting off down the wrong road. It was because of him that he'd joined up and he respected him more than any other person he knew.

Sally was waiting for him and quickly took him to the ICU. "How is he?" he asked as they rushed through the corridors.

"He's been very lucky. We got to him fast," Sally told him, struggling to keep up. "It looks like he's going to be okay."

Relief poured through his veins but he wanted to see for himself. Approaching the nurse at the station outside the chief's room, he asked if he could go in. She looked like she was going to say no but at a nod from Sally changed her mind. "Okay, but only five minutes, and keep the noise down. His wife is in there with him."

Gently pushing open the door he entered the room, immediately struck by how much older and weaker the chief looked. Going to his wife, he gave her a hug before taking a seat next to the bed. The chief was awake and he smiled weakly at him.

"You'll do anything for a day off work, won't you, boss?" he tried to joke.

"I think I'll need more than a day off this time, kid."

Finn tried not to show his concern. "You take as long as you need."

"Bring me up to date on the case. Anything new since last night?"

"The full forensics report came in this morning. Nothing helpful, though."

"You need to try and talk to the boy again, see if he can give us anything."

"Agreed. Without something to go on we're at a dead end. I'll try and talk to him again today and I'll let you know if he says anything helpful."

"No, you won't." It was the chief's wife who spoke this time, surprising them both. "He is under strict instructions to rest, Finn, and I intend to make sure that's exactly what he does."

Finn and the chief exchanged a look; they both knew better than to try and argue with her.

"Unfortunately, Finn, this does mean that you're in charge for now. As of now, you're acting chief."

Finn had known it was coming, but he still grumbled "Okay, but only until you come back. You know I hate the idea of all that responsibility." And he did. He liked to be able to just do his job without having to worry about budgets and politics.

"You'll be fine, Finn. You're a great cop. Just follow your instincts."

"And you're a great chief, so just make sure you rest and get better soon." Saying his goodbyes, he left the room, closing the door before leaning back against it.

The timing couldn't have been any worse. This case had the potential to be an absolute nightmare and now, with the chief out of action, it was all on him. The important thing though was that the chief was going to be okay and he was right; he was a good cop and he had years of experience. Now it was time to put them into action.

Ten

Kat had sat in the back seat of the car with him on the way home. She could already see the change in him. Cleaned up and in new clothes, he didn't look like the same boy she'd found by the side of the road.

"Kat, why don't you show Daniel around, but just don't go in Jake's room. There's something I want to do. I won't be long," Jamie said as soon as they walked through the front door.

Mystified, Kat watched as Jamie disappeared up the stairs. "Looks like it's just you and me then." She smiled at Daniel who was looking around the hall taking it all in.

"Is this all yours?"

"Actually, it's Jamie's. But this is where I was born and grew up. So, do you want to have a look around?" He nodded enthusiastically.

"Okay, let's go!"

Kat was just showing him around the garden when Jamie called down to her.

"You can come up now!"

Climbing the stairs, they made their way to Jake's room where Jamie was standing, looking pleased with herself.

"Oh, Jamie!"

Jamie had obviously been hard at work while she was showing Daniel around and had turned Jake's old room into a room perfect for a young boy. There were posters on the wall and teddies on the bed and the closets had all been cleared out to make room.

"Thank you!" she told her, hugging her close, the tears spilling over.

"No need to thank me." Jamie replied. "He deserves it."

She nodded. "Yes, he does." She looked down to where Daniel was clutching her hand. "So, what do you think, Daniel? Do you like your new room?"

He just nodded, which was all that Kat expected. Though he had spoken to her so she knew that he could, he still didn't seem comfortable enough to do it very often. It worried her that he may have questions that he just didn't feel brave enough to ask yet. There was one question that he hadn't asked, though, that she needed to answer for him anyway. Knowing that she couldn't put it off, she took a deep breath and smiled at him. "I'll tell you what, why don't we go downstairs and get some milk and cookies?"

Leaving Jamie to take him to the living room, Kat went to the kitchen. She needed a minute to gather her thoughts and her strength. She'd delivered death notifications before and it never got any easier, but this was different. This was telling a small child who had already been through so much that he had lost his family, too. She didn't want to; she wanted him to have a bit of happiness back in his life before she took it away from him again, but she had to. She couldn't let him hope that they were coming for him and snatch it away from him again. Pouring milk into a glass and putting some cookies onto a plate, she took them through to the living room.

He'd finished eating and was now sitting on the couch in between the two of them. Turning slightly so that she was facing him, she took his hands in hers.

"Daniel, you've been such a brave boy, but I'm afraid I have to tell you some bad news. I'm so sorry." She took a deep breath. "How much do you remember about your parents, honey?"

He hung his head. "They gave me away." It came out as no more than a whisper.

Kat was shocked. *What?* "No! Sweetheart, they didn't give you away!"

He nodded fiercely. "They did. The boss said they didn't want me anymore." Tears ran down his cheeks.

Kat felt her heart break. "Oh, honey, he lied. Your parents never gave you away. In fact, they never stopped looking for you." She saw a flicker of hope in his eyes and could have kicked herself. "They never stopped, honey, but I'm so sorry. They had an accident a little while ago and there were both killed." Kat held her breath as she waited for a reaction.

He didn't say anything for a moment and then, "They were looking for me?"

She squeezed his hands. "Yes, sweetheart, until the day they died."

His face crumpled then and the sobs came, deep wracking sobs that shook his little body, and he threw himself into her arms. She held him tightly, letting them come, her own tears wetting the hair on the top of his head. Looking over at Jamie who had sat and watched the exchange, she saw that she, too, was distraught and her face was wet with tears.

They sat like that for a while, Kat just holding him while Jamie looked on until, eventually, the sobs were replaced by sniffles and he stopped shaking. Taking his tear-stained face in her hands, she wiped away his tears with her thumbs.

"What about the others?" he whispered.

"The others?" She was confused. "You mean the people that hurt you?" she asked

He shook his head. "No, the other kids. He told us all that our parents didn't want us anymore."

An icy hand clamped itself around her heart. *Others?* "Sweetheart, what other kids do you mean?" She needed to be sure about what he was saying.

"The other kids that were with me. They're still there."

Her whole body felt cold now. "Go and get Finn on the phone. He needs to get over here. Now," she told Jamie, trying to keep her voice calm.

Holding Daniel close while Jamie went to make the call, Kat was scared. *What on earth was going on?* She knew without a doubt, though, that whatever it was, it was much bigger than they'd ever imagined.

Eleven

It felt strange standing at her front door. He'd deliberately avoided Kat for the last six months and now here he was seeking her out. He only just got back from the hospital and had turned around and rushed over as soon as he'd received the garbled call from Jamie. His mind had been elsewhere, worried about the chief, and it had taken a few seconds for what she was telling him to sink in.

He hoped to God they'd got it wrong, but it tied in with the strange DNA profiles found on his clothes. That there might be more kids like this one out there didn't bear thinking about.

"Hi, Finn." It was Jamie who opened the door, immediately enveloping him in a hug, one that he returned. Whatever issues he may have with Kat, they didn't involve Jamie and since he'd helped with her dramatic rescue earlier in the year, they'd remained firm friends.

"Hi Jamie, how you doing? You look great." And she did. When she'd first come home, she'd been scrawny and beaten and bruised from her pimp and a run in with a serial killer. She looked like a different woman now, standing in front of him. She looked healthy and strong, and she even stood straighter and appeared more confident than he'd ever seen her.

"Thanks! Things are going really well."

She gestured at him to come in. "But come in. You really need to hear what the kid has to say."

He could tell she was shaken as he followed her through the house to the living room. He just hoped Daniel reacted better to him this time or he wouldn't get very far.

He was sitting on the couch next to Kat with his back to the door and he had to walk around so that he was standing in front of them. Grabbing one of the matching chairs, he pulled it closer to the couch, but not close enough to intimidate the kid.

"Hi, Daniel, I'm Finn. Do you remember me?" He could see the boy start to shake, but there was no screaming this time and he nodded at him.

"I'm a friend of Kat's and I'm a pretty nice guy." He looked at Kat for support.

"He's right, honey. He's a really good guy," she agreed.

"Now, Kat here tells me that you've got some stuff that you need to tell me that might help me catch the bad guys." He kept his voice low and gentle. "Is that right?"

More nodding. "There are others," he whispered, his eyes downcast. "Other boys."

"Where you were?"

Daniel nodded.

"Do you know where you were, Daniel?"

A shake of the head. "No."

"Was it the other boys who did this to you?"

Daniel looked up at him and met his eyes for the first time, seeming surprised. "No!" He shook his head hard. "Not them. It was different boys."

Finn was confused. Different boys? What did that mean?

"I'm sorry, Daniel, but I'm a bit confused." He smiled gently "How did you get hurt?"

"I had a fight and I lost. The boss makes us fight against other boys, boys who stay somewhere else."

Finn tried not to let the shock he was feeling show on his face. "Were there many other boys there with you, Daniel?"

He nodded.

"And this man you call the boss, he makes them all fight?"

Another nod.

"Okay, Daniel, you've been really helpful. I think that's enough questions for today." He turned to Kat. "Can I have a word?"

Daniel looked completely drained. Finn watched as he curled up on the couch and Kat covered him with a blanket. Leaving Jamie with him, they went to the kitchen to talk about what they'd heard. At first they were both silent as they processed what Daniel had just told them. It seemed too amazing, too horrifying to be true but neither of them was in any doubt that it was. It had been torture for them listening to it and they could only imagine what it must have been like to live through it.

"So what happens now?" Kat was the first to break the silence.

Finn pulled both his hands down across his face, the sound of them scraping across his stubble loud in the quiet kitchen.

"I don't know. I really don't." He sighed "We have zilch to go on and he can't tell us anything about where he was held."

"At least we know it was somewhere around here. He can't have gotten far in the state he was in," Kat pointed out.

"Yes, but you grew up here, Kat. You know as well as I do that outside of town there is nothing except remote farms and hundreds of square miles of fields. He could have come from anywhere."

"For God's sake, Finn, what's wrong with you? Why are you being so negative? We need to come up with a plan, take some action."

"There is no 'we', Kat. This is on me."

"It involves me too, now. I'll talk to the chief. I'm sure there must be some way I can help."

Maybe she could help, he thought. With the chief in the hospital, they were really short-handed and could use an extra pair.

"The chief is in the hospital, Kat." And he told her what had happened, struggling to maintain his composure.

"I'm so sorry Finn, I had no idea." She placed her hand on his arm.

"You weren't to know." He moved his arm slightly, enough so that her hand fell to the side. "It means that I'm in charge for the time being so, like I said, it's on me." He took a deep breath. "But you're right. I could use the help but you can't do much. You're not a cop anymore."

Kat nodded. "You don't need to remind me of that, but I can still be useful. Just tell me what you need."

He could tell she was desperate to help and he'd seen her with the kid; there was no denying that this meant a lot to her. "Look, I've only just found out about this. Let me get back to the station and get some things organized. Once I've done that I'll be in a better position to know what you can help with, okay?"

"Okay." She cleared her throat. "How have you been anyway? It's been a while since we talked."

"I'm fine. I'd better get back to the station." He cut the conversation short. She hid it quickly but he could see that his abruptness had hurt her and he immediately felt bad. "I'm sorry, Kat, but now is not the time for a catch-up."

"No, you're right. But we do need to talk, Finn. We can't put it off forever."

"I know, and we will. But not now."

Letting himself out of the house, he climbed into his cruiser. What Daniel had just told them changed every assumption he'd made and turned this into a much bigger investigation than it had first appeared to be. He needed a clear head to deal with it, now that the chief was in the hospital. Trying to deal with his personal issues with Kat would have to wait.

Twelve

The boss was not a happy man. His men knew it and were staying out of his way. He couldn't believe they'd let the kid get away. He was a kid, for God's sake, and he'd managed to give three of them the slip.

The kids were only ever taken out when they were to attend an event and they'd just been returning from one of these when the kid had escaped. They'd been driving for hours by the time they arrived back at the farm, and through a combination of tiredness and stupidity, it seemed, his men had failed to take the usual precautions when unloading the boys from the truck. There had been six of them. Two of them had bolted; the other four having been in no state to do so. Unfortunately, in the dark they'd only managed to catch one.

After returning the five remaining boys to their cells, the boss had ordered his men to keep looking for the one who had escaped. He'd made them stay out there all night and they'd only returned at first light, tired, wet and hungry but still empty handed.

He took security very seriously, and despite the chances of an escape happening being very remote, he'd always insisted that the boys were blindfolded when they were taken out of their cells. He was glad of that now and he knew that the kid wouldn't be able to tell the police anything about the farm, but he would be able to tell them about the operation. Up until now, the very fact that such an operation existed had been a secret. That was down to good planning. He never grabbed a kid from the same place twice; but now they would know.

Grinding out his cigarette, he stepped off the porch and scanned the yard. He spotted Clay over by the barn. "Clay! Get over here." Clay was the most trusted of his men, all of whom had been carefully selected for their loyalty and their ability to show a complete lack of humanity in exchange for a good pay check.

"Is everything set for tonight?"

Clay nodded. "Yes, boss, but do you think it's a good idea?" he asked "Shouldn't we wait for a bit until we're sure there isn't any come-back from the kid?"

The boss just looked at him, his eyes like pieces of flint. "I'm sorry. Who makes the decisions round here, you or me?"

"Sorry, boss." Clay quickly apologized.

He would never admit it, but Clay did have a point. It was very unusual to have two fights so close together anyway, but he had a new kid he wanted to try out. And it wasn't like he could just cancel. These events involved a lot of planning and organizing with people travelling from all over the country. If he backed out now it could end up costing him a fortune.

"Don't question me again," he snapped. "Go and double check that everything is ready. We can't afford to have any more fuck-ups."

He watched as Clay went off to do as he was told.

***

The room was full; the air smelled of stale sweat and it was hot, sweltering in fact. It wasn't as if they could open any windows, though; there weren't any. The room felt much smaller than it was due to the fact that it was full. The benches, which had been set up four deep along all four walls, were filled with men excitedly waiting for the show to start and there wasn't a spare seat among them. As each man had filed into the room, Clay had taken their bets and now the excitement was almost at fever pitch.

There was another door on the far side of the room, one that only he and his men were allowed to enter. Deciding it was time to begin, the boss went through it. As soon as he closed the door behind him, the noise from the arena was muted and the bright lights were gone. He stood in a dark, dank corridor lit by a single bulb swinging overhead. The corridor was short and it was only a matter of a few steps until it opened up into another large room. This was different, though, as it was filled with cells on either side. Twelve in total and all of them, except one, was occupied.

As he walked past them, each of the occupants cowered against the back wall, trying to get as far away from him as possible. Stopping in front of the penultimate cell on the left hand side, he took his bunch of keys from his pocket and unlocked the door. "You, out," he barked. He didn't know his name; it wasn't necessary and he didn't care. The kid did as he was told. "Come on, let's not keep your public waiting."

This kid was in better shape than the others. He'd only been with him a couple of weeks and he hadn't fought yet. The boss was counting on his freshness to give him the advantage over his opponent; so much so that he'd wagered more than he usually allowed himself to.

The room erupted in shouts and whistles as he opened the door and pushed the kid in ahead of him. Everyone knew that it was a new kid tonight and they were excited to see how he'd do. He'd been told what was expected of him and told what would happen to him if he let the boss down. He was about eleven years old and looked quite strong for his age. This would be his chance to prove himself.

His opponent was another boy of about the same age, although he was taller and more heavily built. As soon as the whistle blew signaling the start of the fight, the taller kid lashed out with a well-aimed punch to the side of the boy's head, knocking him to his knees.

The boss watched as, dazed and confused, he tried to get up, but before he could, he was struck with a hard kick to the ribs. The loud crack was heard around the room as the boy's ribs broke and the boss frowned. He was clearly going to lose his bet this time. He'd already turned away to leave before the tall boy struck the final blow, this time his foot connecting with the side of his head, rendering him unconscious.

Thirteen

It was afternoon by the time he made it back to the station and the place was empty. Picking up the phone, he called the other four deputies and told them to come in. Two were on duty catching up with their own outstanding calls, and two, the night shift, were at home. They'd grumbled a bit, but once he'd told them that it was important they'd agreed readily.

Once they'd all arrived in the squad room he told them about the chief. The news hit them hard. Though he was the longest serving officer, they were all local men and had known him in some capacity all their lives. He gave them a few minutes to take in the news before telling them about his conversation with Daniel.

"At the moment, all we've got is what this kid is telling us and I believe him. There's no forensics to help us out here so we're going to have to rely on good old-fashioned police work." Speaking to the two officers currently on the night shift, he told them, "We can't have shifts not cover on nights so you'll have to carry on doing that. While it's quiet, though, I want you keeping an eye out to see if you see anything suspicious. Check barns, abandoned farms, anywhere you come across to see if you can find anything." He indicated the door with his thumb. "For now, though, get yourselves back home to bed and get some rest."

He turned his attention back to the other two officers in the room, "Kat McKay is the one who found him and she's offered to help. Normally I wouldn't even consider it, but we're very thin on the ground and she has a lot of experience so I'm going to ask her to look at local property records. Get her to try and narrow down any possible locations for us."

He heard a snicker and looked up from checking his notes. Deputy Carver was the newest recruit to the department. He'd been there for just under a year and Finn had never warmed up to him. He was cocky, arrogant and far too headstrong for his liking. He'd talked to the chief about his concerns about him but he'd just waved them off as being a result of his youth; he was only twenty-two. He'd also pointed out that he reminded him very much of Finn at the same age.

"Anything you'd like to share, Jason?" he asked him now.

He watched as he tried to hide his grin but his mouth got the better of him, as Finn had known it would. "Just that we'll have to take your word about Miss McKay's *experience.*" He snickered again.

Finn sighed. News of Kat's return hadn't taken long to get around town and, as a small community, most people remembered the history between them. Jason's father had been a couple of years older than them but had hung around with the same people. He'd obviously shared the story with his son.

"Deputy Carver, need I remind you that a child has been found, severely beaten, and that other children may be at risk. Right now," the steel in his voice had the desired effect and Jason dropped his head, "I'll thank you to keep your thoughts about my private life to yourself and concentrate on your job. Understood?"

"Yes, sir. Sorry."

"Good. For now we still can't do much more than we've been doing, so for the rest of your shift I want you two doing the same thing. I'll be staying here following up on the information Daniel gave us. Jason, before you go can I have a word?"

He turned and walked into the chief's office leaving Deputy Carver to follow him. "Close the door please."

He waited until the door was closed before he spoke. "For some reason, the chief has faith in you." He paused. "I think that faith is misplaced. But he is the chief so I'll respect that, but if you ever talk to me again like that again I will suspend you on the spot. Am I making myself clear?"

"Yes, sir."

"Good. Now get out there and try and prove me wrong, okay?"

Finn sighed as he watched Carver grab his stuff and leave the office. He hoped that he'd gotten through to him. He needed to trust all his men on the ground right now and he certainly didn't have time to keep an eye on him.

Where to start? Listening to Daniel this morning, he'd been left speechless. If what he was saying was true, and he had no reason to believe it wasn't, then this was a kidnapping ring on a huge scale. It wasn't just the kids that had been locked up with him; he'd described traveling all over the country and seeing countless other kids in the same situation. Something on that scale was for the Feds to deal with, but before he went to them, he needed something to give them. Something more than the word of a scared kid.

The office was empty, so he had a bit of quiet to do some digging. Turning on his computer, he paused for a moment, not sure what to search for. Daniel had told them that some of the kids were younger and some were a bit older, but not my much. He decided to start his search for missing boys between the ages of eight and fourteen, nationwide. *But how far back do I go?* Daniel had been there several years so he decided to go back eight years. The results floored him. *Dear God! What had happened to all these kids?* The list was huge, the names numbering in the hundreds. There was no way they could investigate all those; he needed to narrow the parameters.

Daniel had been able to give them some names. Not all of them as from what he said not all the boys stayed long but there had been half a dozen that had been there with him for the past couple of years. Pulling his notebook out of his pocket, he checked the names that Daniel had given him. Josh, Sam, Tom, Jake, Adam and Tyler. Putting these names into the search results narrowed the list considerably, but there were still over fifty names staring back at him.

Printing it off, he looked at the list. He hated to do it, but he was going to have to ask Daniel to take a look at the photos and see if he recognized any of them.

It could wait until tomorrow, though, he thought as he was overtaken by a huge yawn. He checked his watch and saw that it was past six p.m. He'd been up for two days straight and if he didn't get some sleep he'd be no use to anyone. Besides, after this morning he wanted to give the kid a break. If he pushed too hard there was a danger that what little progress they'd made with him would be lost and he'd clam up. No, it was best that he headed home for some rest. Even just a few hours.

Fourteen

Jamie hadn't wanted to leave Kat and Daniel alone after Finn had left but it was her turn to visit Jake. They took it in turns to go and visit him in the state prison and this week it was her turn. She knew that there were some people in Brecon Point who didn't understand how she'd forgiven him for killing her fiancé. In fact there had been a few resignations at work when she'd taken over. She'd tried to explain to Ted's parents but they hadn't understood and it pained her that they would no longer talk to her. She knew her brother, though, and her faith in him was unswerving. She knew it had been an accident, just as she knew that her own father had partly driven him to it.

The drive to the prison took about two hours but it was a drive that Jamie didn't mind. The prison was located far away from any towns. The journey there took her mostly through the countryside and she enjoyed watching the fields roll past the windows and the country smells on the air.

The first few visits after Jake had been convicted and sentenced had been hard for all of them, the time filled with silences where none of them knew what to say to each other. But now Jake seemed to have adjusted quite well and they'd gotten into a routine with the weekly visits. It was never going to be an enjoyable thing, but it was certainly less traumatic than it had been.

Pulling into the visitor's parking lot, she locked her purse in the glove box before stepping out of the car with nothing but her car keys on her and made her way to the visitors entrance. After the usual search, she was ushered into the visiting room. That term made it sound nicer than it was. In fact, it was a room separated by a partition down the middle. The partition was split into individual sections of glass with a chair in front of each section. The visitors entered through one door on one side of the glass, and the prisoners entered through another on the other side. What looked like telephone handsets were available on each side to talk through.

Sitting down with the other visitors, she waited until the door opened and the prisoners were led in. She smiled as Jake walked in behind another prisoner and took his seat opposite her before lifting the handset.

"Hey, bro, good to see you."

"You too, sis."

As usual, Jamie did most of the talking. He was always desperate for news of the outside world and she always made sure it was cheerful and upbeat. She had thought long and hard about telling him about Daniel on the way up here but had decided against it for now; it wasn't exactly a happy subject.

"Jake, are you listening to me?" He looked distracted, staring into space as if she wasn't there.

"What? Sorry, what were you saying?"

"Jake, what's wrong? You're not yourself today at all." He'd been quiet since she walked in and didn't seem interested in what she was telling him. He seemed about to tell her something when one of the guards walked past and he quickly closed his mouth and said nothing.

"Jake? What is it?" She watched as he checked where the guard was before seeming to hunch himself over the mouthpiece.

"I'm okay. But Jamie, listen to me. If anything happens to me it won't have been an accident."

Jamie was complete taken aback. "What do you mean if something happens to you?"

"Shhhhh! Keep it down, would you?" He was looking around him, making sure no one could overhear. "Just remember what I said, okay?"

The guard chose that moment to tell them visiting time was over and to wrap it up.

Jamie watched, dumbstruck, as Jake put the handset down and blew her a kiss with a small smile before getting in line and filing out of the room with the other prisoners.

What the hell was that all about? She thought as she collected her car keys and made her way out to the parking lot. Part of her wanted to go back inside and demand that she be allowed to see him and get to the bottom of it, but she knew full well that they wouldn't allow it. Also, something about the way he had looked at the guard told her it wouldn't be a good idea.

She couldn't enjoy the countryside on her way home. She couldn't stop thinking about what Jake had said and what he could possibly have meant by it. Usually, on the way home from these visits she stopped at a diner she passed on the way and had a coffee. It had become a bit of a routine for her and one she looked forward to. Today, though, she just wanted to get home and drove straight past. She would talk to Kat and see what she thought.

Fifteen

After Finn had gone and Jamie had set off for the weekly visit to Jake there was just the two of them. Daniel had slept for two hours curled up on the sofa and Kat had curled up in the chair next to him with a strong cup of coffee and watched over him.

Her lack of ability to do anything was bothering her and she was feeling irritable. For the first time since handing in her badge, she was wishing that she hadn't, that she could be more involved with the investigation. Just sitting in the wings while others worked the case didn't sit well with her at all. She sighed. There was nothing she could do about it, she just had to hope that Finn would let her do something. *Finn.* She'd given him space, not wanting to push him and hadn't sought him out when it had become clear that he'd been avoiding her but seeing him with Sally at the hospital, she wondered if she'd done the wrong thing.

Daniel stirred on the couch, interrupting her thoughts. "Hey, sleepy."

He smiled as soon as he saw her.

"How are you feeling?"

"Okay, but I'm hungry."

"Well then, young man, best we feed you then!"

Holding his hand, she took him into the kitchen in search of lunch. She'd already made up her mind that he'd gone through enough for one day and that she wasn't going to try and get any more information from him. Her priority now was to get him settled in and to work on making him feel safe.

Undoubtedly he'd missed a huge part of his childhood, so after lunch they went into the dining room and covered the table with sheets. After rummaging around for a bit, Kat managed to find some paints and they spent the rest of the afternoon happily making as much of a mess as they could. He even laughed a couple of times and Kat was sure this was a sign they were making progress.

By the time Jamie got home from visiting Jake, he had relaxed a bit and was no longer following her from room to room, quite content to be left in the living room watching TV as long as he knew where she was.

"What a day." Kat sighed as she came downstairs after seeing Daniel safely tucked in bed. Taking the well-deserved glass of wine that Jamie held out to her, they both went to sit in the living room. Letting the couch envelop her, she took a sip from the glass and groaned. "God, I needed that today. So, how was the visit? Was Jake okay?"

Jamie twirled her glass in her hand looking thoughtful. "Well, to be honest, it was strange." She looked up. "He really wasn't his usual self and then, just before I left, he said something that really worried me."

"What?"

"He said that if anything happened to him that it wouldn't be an accident."

"Okay, that's odd. Did he say anything else?"

"He didn't have chance. That was right at the end of the visit."

Jamie looked worried and Kat had to admit she was, too, now. "Well, there's nothing we can do right now, especially as we don't have any idea what he was talking about. It's my turn to visit next week so I'll see if I can get anything more out of him."

They spent the rest of the evening talking about Daniel, but both of them were worn out and exhaustion soon got the better of them. After saying good night to Jamie, Kat went upstairs to check on Daniel before turning in herself. He was sleeping soundly, cuddling one of the teddies they'd put in his room and the sight made Kat's breath catch in her throat. Closing the door gently, so as not to disturb him, she made her way to her own room and gratefully fell into bed.

***

Something had woken her. Remaining still and trying to control her breathing so she could hear clearly, she listened. Nothing. She must have imagined it. Flipping her pillow to the cold side, she rolled over and that's when she saw him. He was curled up on the floor next to her bed, fast asleep. It was a sight that brought an immediate lump to her throat. It must have been the sound of him coming into her room that had disturbed her on some level. There was no way she was going to just leave him there, but he obviously didn't want to be alone. She chided herself for not thinking about that. In a strange house with strange people, of course he didn't want to be alone.

Quietly pushing the covers aside, she climbed out of bed. He was so small and thin that it was an easy task to lift him and put him in her own bed and she was pleased she managed to do it without waking him. She pulled the covers over him before dropping a kiss on his forehead. Grabbing herself a spare blanket, she wrapped herself in it and curled up in the wingback chair she had positioned near the bedroom window

The moon was almost full tonight and lit the room with a glow. Resting her head back against the chair, Kat looked out of the window across the gardens at the back of the house. Her thoughts inevitably drifted to Finn. *Had she done the right thing telling him?* Yes. She was wrong not to tell him at the time but she'd been not much more than a kid.

The closeness that had started to develop between them though when she'd come back after all those years had scared her and she'd known that if there was to be any future for them then she needed to be honest. It had been one of the hardest things she'd ever had to do, telling him about his son. The son he never knew he had. Her father had made it clear; his daughter was not going to be an unmarried mother, nor would he allow her to marry beneath her. She'd been given a choice. Get rid of the baby or leave.

She could still remember that day as if it were yesterday. Her mother had stood behind him in the living room, sobbing, but doing nothing to stand up for her. She already knew that she would rather die than get rid of the baby so he'd sealed her fate. Yes, she'd considered telling Finn then but she knew he had dreams of college, of a bright future. They'd talked about it often enough and she had no doubt that he would do it. She loved him; how could she stand in his way? She couldn't tell him because he was honorable and would have stood by her; she couldn't let him do that. So she'd packed her bags that night and left town without so much as a goodbye.

She looked over at where Daniel was sleeping soundly. Her son would be much older than he was now. She couldn't turn back time and change the decisions she had made, but she could do everything she could for this child, this small boy who had wormed his way into her heart from the first minute she'd laid eyes on him. Feeling her eyelids start to droop, she closed her eyes and let herself drift back off to sleep.

Sixteen

She'd woken when the sun had risen above the horizon and its rays had landed on her eyelids, teasing her awake. Jamie had already been up when she'd gone down to the kitchen, leaving Daniel asleep in her bed.

"Morning," Kat mumbled.

"Morning. How did you sleep? You look tired."

"Sleeping in a chair will do that to you." She explained what had happened during the night.

"Poor little thing." Jamie handed her a coffee fresh from the pot. "He'll settle in, Kat. It just might take a little bit of time."

"I know. Listen, I was thinking. Obviously, I can't go into the office and leave Daniel alone for the time being so I was thinking, if it's okay with you, I'll pop in later today and grab some stuff and do some work from home."

"You don't have to do that, Kat. We can cover things for now."

"I know, but I want to," Kat insisted.

"If you're sure, then of course it's okay with me."

"Okay, I'll swing by later."

"Okay. Well, I'd better get going. Give him a hug from me."

She was just finishing her coffee when she heard him come downstairs. "I'm in the kitchen!" she called out, not wanting him to panic and think he was alone.

"I'm just going to make breakfast," she told him as he walked in rubbing his eyes. "Pancakes okay?"

"Yes, please."

They ate in silence, though Daniel didn't eat much. He was used to barely being fed so it was hardly surprising; she knew it would take time to build up his appetite again.

"You all done?" she asked before clearing his breakfast plate, stacking it in the dishwasher and turning it on. "Do you feel up to a short trip into town today?"

He nodded.

She knew he needed to take it easy but getting him out of the house might also do him so good.

"Okay, good. I'll tell you what, the coffee shop in town makes great milkshakes so we'll go and get one." She reached for her cell. "Now, you go and wash up and get out of you pj's. I've just got to make a quick call."

She waited until he'd left the room before dialing Finn's number. It only rang once before he picked up.

"Hi, Finn, it's Kat" She knew he'd let her know if there had been any developments but she wanted to check in and let him know what she had planned. "Any news?"

"No." She heard him sigh heavily. "Has he said anything else to you, Kat? Anything at all that might give us more to go on?"

"I would have called you if he had," she chided gently.

"The night shift had a poke around last night and didn't spot anything, but there's so much ground to cover. If we just had an idea where to start!"

"Did you think about what I said? Is there anything I can do to help?"

"Actually, yes. Do you think you could have a look at the local land records, see if you can see anything unusual? The kind of operation the kid is describing, there just has to be some kind of a trail."

"Yep, of course I'd be glad to help. I've told Daniel that I'll take him into town this morning for a treat so I'll pop in to grab them first and bring them back here to go over. Can you contact them and let them know it's okay?"

"Yep, will do. And thanks, Kat."

Seventeen

He'd barely said a word in the car. She'd driven to the office and grabbed some files to take home and work on and then headed straight into town. Kat felt her heart squeeze in her chest as she glanced over at him. He had been through so much. The physical injuries would heal, she knew, but the psychological scars undoubtedly ran deep and those were the ones that were worrying her right now. Apart from sleeping by the side of her bed, he seemed to be coping well. Too well. So much pain needed an outlet. Thankfully, his first session with the therapist was scheduled for that evening. It was going to take a lot of time and love to get him through this and she had every intention of making sure he got whatever he needed.

Finding a parking spot outside the town hall, they made their way inside. The building was on the main street through Brecon Point and was only a few doors down from the police station. With Daniel holding her hand, she spoke to the clerk who confirmed that Finn had contacted them and authorized them to let her take some of the property records home. She'd had to sign her life away, in triplicate, to do so but it meant that she didn't have to make Daniel sit there for hours with her while she went through them. Thankfully, the box wasn't that large and, with a bit of effort and with Daniel opening the doors, she was able to get it into the trunk of her car without too much difficulty.

"Okay then, young man. How about that trip to the coffee shop I promised you?" she asked after the car was all locked up again. It was only a few hundred yards down the street and there was no point moving the car so they walked hand in hand, with Kat introducing him to the town as they went.

Eighteen

He'd hoped the boy would be found dead in the woods. He'd suffered quite a beating at the last match and he'd hoped that that, combined with the fact that he was very weak anyway, would have assured that he didn't make it. But he'd just been told that not only was he still alive but he'd been found and taken to the police. He was furious. Nothing like this had ever happened before and now, because of a stupid mistake by one of his men, the whole operation was in jeopardy.

"What has he told them?" he demanded of the person on the other end of the phone. His hand gripped the phone tightly; his next move depended on the answer to his question.

"Nothing. I mean, obviously he's told them about the operation but he hasn't told them anything that could lead them to you. He doesn't know anything to tell them, does he?"

"No." He wracked his brain to try and think if there was anything at all he could tell them that would lead them back to him but he couldn't think of anything.

"Okay, keep me updated." He disconnected the call, dropping the phone on the kitchen table in disgust. He could lose everything and it all depended on whether the boy knew anything or not. Who knew what he could have overheard that could give them just the clue they needed to get back to him? That thought made him angrier than he ever thought possible.

Looking around, he took in the kitchen which had barely changed in sixty years. Even the cabinets were the same ones that had been there throughout his childhood. This farm had been in his family for decades and now he could lose it all.

There was only one thing to do. The boy. He couldn't leave him out there. Although he didn't think he knew anything, he wasn't absolutely sure. No, he was a loose end that needed to be dealt with, and soon.

Nineteen

They were sitting in the coffee shop, enjoying the milkshake she'd promised him, when her phone rang. Smiling at Daniel, she checked the screen and saw that it was Finn. Hoping for news, she answered quickly.

"Hey, Kat, are you still in town or are you back home already?"

"We're across the road having a milkshake."

She listened as he explained about what he had discovered so far and about the pictures he wanted Daniel to have a look through.

"I'm not sure, Finn." She looked at where Daniel was concentrating hard on his drink and lowered her voice. "I'm not sure how he'll take it."

She heard him sigh on the other end of the phone. "I know, Kat, and believe me, if I didn't have to I wouldn't even ask. I hate the idea of putting him through any more but it could help and at this point we need all the help we can get."

She knew he was right but it tore at her heart to have to put him through any more distress. But they had no choice; they needed to find out as much as they could about the monster who had done this. Agreeing to meet him at the station after they'd finished up, she put the phone away and turned her attention back to Daniel.

"Are you enjoying that?" She smiled, taking in the milky moustache that he now sported on his top lip. He just nodded and concentrated on scooping the foam from the bottom of the glass with a long handled spoon. "I'm just gonna go to the bathroom, okay?" She pointed to the door on the other side of the shop. "It's just over there". Daniel had to twist in his chair and look behind him to see where she was pointing. "Is that okay?"

"Yeah."

Sliding out of the booth, Kat headed for the bathroom, turning as she got near to check on him over her shoulder. She needn't have worried; the milkshake had his complete attention.

"Watch where you're going, will ya!" she heard as she walked into a man coming out of the bathroom, the collision nearly knocking her off her feet. He was huge, over six feet tall and nearly as wide by the looks of it. He was scowling at her angrily.

Kat held up her hands. "I'm so sorry. I wasn't watching where I was going."

"No kidding." He sneered before walking away and out of the front door.

It was an accident, dumbass, Kat thought as she watched him leave before heading into the bathroom.

Twenty

He was still slightly nervous around Finn and held Kat's hand tightly, but he seemed to understand now that he wasn't a threat. Sitting Daniel at his desk, Finn crouched down on his haunches in front of him, bringing himself down to his level.

"Daniel, you've been so brave so far and we're all really proud of you. I'm afraid, though, that I need to ask you to be brave for a bit longer. Do you think you can do that for me?"

He watched as he looked up at where Kat was standing just behind him with her hand on his shoulder as she nodded at him encouragingly.

"Yes," he answered in a quiet voice.

"Okay, I've got some pictures in a book that I want you to look at. All I want you to do is point if you recognize any of them, okay?"

Standing up, he gently turned Daniel's chair to face the desk and opened the book of photographs that was sitting in front of him.

The tension was palpable as the only sound in the room was of the pages of the book turning. After turning several pages, Daniel silently pointed to a photo. Finn didn't speak as he silently took a note of the number in the top right hand corner of the image, nodding

encouragingly at him. It took several minutes for him to
go through the book and by the time he had finished, he
had pointed to seven images.

"Thank you, Daniel." He looked at where Kat was
standing with one hand on Daniel's shoulder and could
see she was as shocked as he was by the number of
pictures he'd pointed out. "Daniel, were all these boys
there when you left?" he asked gently.

Daniel shook his head and opened the book again.
Quickly flicking through, he pointed to two photos.
"Only them."

"Okay Daniel. You've been fantastic." He could see
that he was starting to get distressed now, though.
"We're all done here."

He turned to Kat. "Did you get those property
records okay?"

She nodded. "Yep. They're in the trunk of my car
and I'll start going through them as soon as I can. Is
there anything in particular you want me to look for or
am I just looking for anything unusual?"

He thought about that for a moment. "To be honest,
I don't know. Anything that stands out, trust your gut
Kat. You know what you're doing."

"Okay, well I'll let you know if I find anything. For
now, though, this little guy is worn out and it's time I
got back." She gave Finn a small smile. "Let me know if
there's any news."

Twenty-One

It was early afternoon by the time they pulled up in front of the house. Jamie's car was parked outside and Kat was pleased that she was home early for a change. Since taking over the family business, she was working hard, long hours to prove herself and Kat worried that she may overdo it. Today, though, she was pleased she was there because she needed to unload. It had been an emotionally exhausting day, for her and Daniel, and she needed to let off some steam.

Gently telling him to go and watch some TV, she went looking for Jamie, finding her in the kitchen making some fresh coffee.

"Hey, you're home early," she said, sliding onto a kitchen stool and resting her arms on the countertop.

"Yeah, I couldn't seem to focus with everything that's going and thought maybe you might need me here. Coffee?"

Kat nodded gratefully. "Please."

Nothing more was said as Kat watched Jamie prepare the coffee, finding the simple actions comforting. She was so proud of her; she had come such a long way since she had come back to them and looking at her now, you would never believe she had suffered so much.

Placing a mug in front of Kat, Jamie hopped on to the stool next to her. "So tell me about today."

So she did. From the moment they left this morning to when they got home, Kat told her everything. As she talked, she found some of the tension leaving her shoulders. It was good to get it out. "The hardest thing is not being able to do anything! All those poor kids out there somewhere and we don't know where."

"How did Daniel do?"

"He was amazing. He picked out the pictures of the boys he recognized. The worrying thing is that some were there with him, but then they just disappeared and never came back." She took a deep breath. "But he handled it really well. He seems to be coping, but its early days. It could be that it hasn't all really hit him yet."

"And how were things with Finn?"

Kat could see the concern on Jamie's face. Not long after she'd told Finn her secret she'd also told Jamie, who had been incredibly supportive. She'd been scared that she would judge her for what she'd done but she hadn't. Instead she'd encouraged her to talk about it and was always ready to listen. She shrugged now in answer to her question. "Strained I think is the best way to describe it." She sighed. "I know I've no right to expect anything from him, but I'd hoped he might have been ready to talk about it by now." The truth was, she'd hoped for more, maybe even a future together, but the fact that he was dating someone told her that that was never going to happen and it was something she was just going to have to learn to accept.

"Do you want me to talk to him?"

"God, no. No, this has to come from him." And if it never did, that was something she was going to have to accept, too.

Jamie stood up. "Okay. Well I'm sure you're both hungry because I know I am so why don't you go and spend a bit of time with that gorgeous boy in there and I'll rustle us up some dinner."

Kat checked her watch. "Okay good idea. We need to eat early tonight because Daniel's got his first appointment with his therapist today. We've got to be there at seven."

"Couldn't they have seen you during the day?"

"Absolutely, but it would have meant waiting for at least two weeks for an appointment. This way, he can be seen right away. I don't want to leave it any longer than I have to. He's got so much to deal with."

"Your right, it's definitely best to get him seen right away." Jamie started opening cupboard doors. "I'll fix us some pasta, that's quick. Now go sit down and relax. I'll call you when it's ready."

Gratefully, Kat did as she was told.

Twenty-Two

Finn sat looking at the pictures that Daniel had picked out. He'd hoped that he would pick out one, maybe two. He'd never dreamed he would pick out seven. Out of the seven, only two had still been there when Daniel had escaped. The other four had all been there with him at some point, but not recently. There were also many, many other boys that had been there, and were there, but whose photos were not in the book. Still, it was somewhere to start.

Taking the two photos that he'd chosen out of the book, he turned them over. Sam and Adam. By inputting their full details into the computer, he was able to view their missing person reports. Both boys had been reported missing within the last six years. One, Sam, had been reported missing just over two years ago. He'd been visiting the mall with his grandmother when she'd lost sight of him. He hadn't been seen again since. The other boy, Adam, had been reported missing nearly four years ago. This time, he'd been in the park playing with a group of friends and their mothers and somehow he'd vanished. Apart from both vanishing within the last six years, they were both of roughly the same age. Sam had just turned seven and Adam vanished shortly before his seventh birthday. The similarities ended there, though.

Geographically, they were over five hundred miles apart and both boys came from very different backgrounds.

In each case, the families had been looked at closely but there had never been any indication that they'd been involved.

Making a note of the contact details for the police departments handling each of the cases, he contacted them. He was in luck and managed got get hold of the original investigating officers in both cases and he explained why he was interested in their cases. Happy to help, both officers agreed to send a copy of their case files to him by overnight mail.

Finn wasn't sure what he hoped to find but maybe now, knowing that they were in fact connected and not separate incidents, something might jump out at him.

Sandy, the department receptionist, office manager and general organizational guru popped her head around the door. "I'm off, Finn. See you in the morning."

Surprised, Finn checked his watch and realized that it was after five. There was nothing more he could do tonight and he'd planned to cook for Sally that evening before this case had landed on his desk. He considered calling her and putting it off but decided not to. It would do him good to get away from the office for a bit and he enjoyed her company, so it might take his mind of things for a bit.

When he'd told Kat that he needed time to process the bombshell she'd dropped on him, he'd meant it. He certainly hadn't set out to meet someone and start dating.

Putting the book aside, he left the office. It felt good to think about something other than the case for a bit as he thought about what he was going to cook for dinner on the way home. He knew the contents of his fridge were limited and he hadn't had time to go to the store in days, so it would take a bit of creativity on his part. Checking his fridge when he arrived confirmed his fears. Steak and baked potatoes it would have to be.

The doorbell rang just as he was taking the potatoes out of the oven. "Perfect timing," he said as he let her in. "I'm afraid it's nothing fancy."

"Believe me, when you've just worked a shift like the one I've had you could feed me a bag of hay and I'd be happy." She laughed. "Smells good, whatever it is."

The evening was dry and clear so they took their food out onto the deck to watch the sun go down as they ate.

"Much better than a bag of hay, thank you," she said when she'd finished and pushed her plate aside.

"So, tell me about you and Kat McKay."

Finn paused with his fork halfway to his mouth. "What do you mean?"

"Well, at the hospital the other day, there was a definite vibe between you. History?"

He decided to be honest. "Well yes, but not in the way you think." He put his fork down. "We dated in high school."

"And she's still not over it?"

"No, it's not like that." She listened intently as he told her all about what had happened with Jamie and what had ultimately brought Kat back into his life. He drew short of telling her about Kat's secret; that wasn't his to tell and it would feel like a betrayal to share it with anyone else.

"So what made you pick this area of the country to work in?" He turned the tables on her. Though they'd been on a few dates, she'd shared very little of her own life before arriving here.

"You mean besides the bright lights and non-stop city life?" she chuckled. "I don't know, really. It seemed like a good idea at the time and now," she looked into his eyes, "it seems like an even better one."

"So you don't have family around here?"

She laughed. "Why, do you want to meet them already?"

He pulled a face in mock horror. "Gosh no," he chuckled. "It just seems a bit of an odd place to choose. Most people haven't even heard of Brecon Point."

"I get the best of both worlds here. I get to be the friendly town doctor some of the time, and the ER doctor the rest of the time. What's not to love?"

"It must be hard, though, moving to a new town where you don't know anyone," he persisted.

"Like I said, best of both worlds." She stood up. "So, are you going to show me this car of yours then?"

I guess that's the end of that conversation, Finn thought as he stood up to take her through to the garage.

Twenty-Three

The dark road stretched ahead for miles with nothing to break the monotony. It got dark early at this time of year and it was only just past six p.m., but being completely surrounded by darkness gave the feeling that it was the middle of the night. Daniel was asleep on the back seat so there wasn't a sound in the car other than the wheels turning on the road. She didn't want to turn the radio on as she didn't want to wake him. They were on their way back from his first therapy session and it had clearly drained him as he'd fallen asleep almost as soon as she'd driven out of the center's parking lot.

The therapist was one that was recommended by CPS and she had seemed very warm and welcoming. She'd insisted that Kat wait outside while she talked to Daniel alone, so she'd sat in the waiting room anxiously, hoping it was going well. She had no idea what had been said, but when Daniel had emerged at the end of his session and the therapist had asked him if he wanted to come again, he had said that yes, he would.

A sudden flash of light in the darkness made her close her eyes briefly and she looked around, confused as to where it was coming from. Looking in her mirror, she realized that while she'd been lost in thought a car had appeared on the road behind her and it appeared to have its high beams on. *Idiot,* she thought as she adjusted her mirror so that the glare didn't blind her.

The bump when it came shocked her. *What the hell?* Checking her mirror again, she realized that the car she'd seen behind her had sped up and was now inches from her trunk. *Had he just hit her?* As she watched, it sped up and hit her car again, the jolt harder this time and throwing her forward against her seatbelt.

"What's happening?"

The impacts had woken Daniel up and he was now looking out the back window fearfully.

"I don't know, honey." Whatever was going on she knew one thing for sure. It wasn't good. She was on a deserted stretch of road, after dark, with a child in the car being rammed by God knows who. Putting her foot down, she sped up, keeping an eye in her mirror as she pulled away. Whoever was driving the car, though, matched her increase in speed and was quickly right back to where he was. *Shit. Shit. Shit.*

Keeping one hand firmly on the wheel, she reached over to the passenger seat with the other. She'd put her purse there when she'd gotten in the car and now, sliding her hand inside, she rummaged round for her cell. She quickly found it, her hand touching its smooth surface and took it out. One handed, she dialed 911 and held the phone to her ear. Silence. A quick glance at the screen told her that there was no cell service. *Dammit!* The next jolt made her lose her grip on the phone and sent it flying onto the floor. She knew that whatever happened she just had to keep going; she had no idea who was in the car or why they were doing this but if she stopped there would be no getting away from them, whatever their intentions were. This thought had no sooner entered her brain when the car was hit again. This time, though, they had inched alongside and hit the car sideways. "Hold on!" she screamed as they were pushed into a spin. There was nothing she could do except hold on to the steering wheel as the car spun out of control, leaving the road and crashing into a ditch that ran alongside. The car teetered on two wheels for a moment before settling back on all four wheels with a crash and a grinding of metal. In shock and breathing heavily, she just sat for what seemed like an age before quickly turning in her seat.

"Are you okay, honey?" she asked Daniel, visually checking him over for injuries. Thankfully, he had none, though he was clearly terrified. Scrambling for her belt, she quickly undid it but before she could get out of the car the back door was flung open and a pair of arms reached in.

"What are you doing?" she screamed as she saw them reach for Daniels belt. "Stop!" Flinging her door open, she leapt from the car only to be grabbed from behind by another pair of strong arms that quickly wrapped around her and held her tight. "Let go of me! What are you doing? Stop!" She struggled against the arms as she watched the other man pull Daniel out of the car. "Nooo!" she screamed again as she watched him being dragged out of the ravine and up towards the road.

"Kat!"

The scream cut to her core and filled her with renewed strength. Bending her knee and raising her leg, she kicked back with all her strength and was rewarded by a satisfying crunch as her shoe made contact with bone.

The man cried out in pain, his arms releasing her as he clutched at his now shattered kneecap. Without looking back, she scrambled up the bank towards where Daniel was now being forced into the back of the car that had rammed them. The man pushing him into the car was standing with his back to her as he pushed Daniel into the back seat and with a hard kick, she struck the back of his right knee which immediately gave way, causing him to drop to his knees. Her years of training in the LAPD kicked in and she lashed out again, this time connecting with the side of his head as he was kneeling, the blow sending him flying onto his back where he lay motionless.

"Daniel, come on honey, quick!" she shouted to him where he sat cowering in the back seat of the car.

He didn't move fast enough, though, and the driver of the car reacted quickly, throwing open his door and getting out. As he stood up, his eyes met Kat's across the roof of the car and recognition hit her. *She'd seen him before!* "You're the guy from the coffee shop!"

Moving quickly, she reached into the back seat and grabbed Daniel by the hand, pulling him towards her. It was all the time he needed, and before she could get him out of the car the driver was by her side. The stab of pain in her neck was completely unexpected and immediately she felt her knees give way before crumpling onto the ground beside the open door. She stayed conscious long enough to see his big hands reaching down toward her before her world went black.

Twenty-Four

Jamie was worried. They should have been back hours ago. She'd called the clinic, thinking maybe they had been delayed, but the office was closed. Calls to Kat's cell had gone straight to voicemail and, despite leaving several increasing worried messages, she'd failed to call her back. Something was wrong and she'd waited long enough. Picking up the phone, she dialed Finn's number. It seemed to ring for ages as she paced up and down in the kitchen, keeping one eye on the window in case Kat's car suddenly appeared, but at last he picked up.

"Hi, Jamie," he answered.

"Finn, something's wrong." She didn't waste any time with niceties.

"What do you mean something's wrong? What's happened?"

"It's Kat. She took Daniel to the therapist's office ages ago and she hasn't come home."

There was a silence on the end of the phone. "Have you tried her cell?"

"Of course I've tried her cell!" she snapped.

"Okay, look, it's probably nothing. You know what the cell signal is like around here. She's probably broken down at the side of the road or got a flat."

He was right. Of course he was right, Jamie told herself. She was being paranoid. "Okay, you're right. Well, I'm going to go and retrace her steps, then, and see if I can find her."

"No, you stay there in case she comes home. I'll get a couple of the guys to go and do it. You'll see. She'll be home in no time. I'll let you know as soon as we've found her, okay?"

Looking out the window with the now silent phone in her hand, Jamie tried to relax but she couldn't. She wouldn't. Not until she saw her safe and sound for herself.

Twenty-Five

Though he'd tried to reassure Jamie when she'd called, he'd immediately had a bad feeling when she'd told him that Kat hadn't made it home. She was a very capable woman and if she'd had a flat she would have been more than able to change it herself. Yes, she could have broken down, but her car was new and it seemed unlikely. Making his apologies to Sally, he'd left her at his house and immediately joined the search.

The police radio in his cruiser crackled to life and Jason's voice came over the air. "I've found the car. It's on the top road, about five miles out from Brecon Point." Finn held his breath. "There's no one with it."

Cursing, Finn put his foot down. *That didn't sound good.* He was there in a matter of minutes. Jason was leaning against the door of his cruiser, smoking, when Finn pulled up alongside. "Put that out. You're on duty," he told him as he stepped out of his car.

He watched as Jason shrugged and dropped the cigarette to the ground before grinding it out with his shoe. Satisfied, he turned and gingerly made his way down the bank to where he could see Kat's car in the gloom, almost invisible from the road. "Well-spotted," he said to Jason, who had followed him down the bank and now stood next to him. "How did you spot it from the road?"

He just shrugged. "Just lucky, I guess."

The driver's door of the car was open, as was one of the back doors, and there was extensive damage to the trunk and to the driver's side. But Jason was right; there was no sign of Kat or Daniel. Crouching down, Finn pulled his flashlight from his belt and pointed the beam at the damage. There, clearly visible, were flecks of red paint. "Get on to CSI and get them out here." He indicated the red paint with his flashlight. "Whatever happened here, another vehicle was involved."

Next he turned his attention to the inside of the car, noting that Kat's purse was still there, its contents scattered over the passenger floor, including her cell. Slipping on a pair of latex gloves he retrieved from his pocket, he carefully picked it up, being careful not to disturb anything else. Standing up, he quickly flicked through her call logs and noted the 911 call. It appeared that it hadn't connected and he saw that the phone wasn't picking up any service. Any doubt that this had been a deliberate act vanished.

There were no obvious signs of any blood which was good news. He had to hope that wherever they were, they were uninjured. The alternative didn't bear thinking about. Instructing Jason to stay at the scene, he made his way back up the bank to his own car. He needed to go and break the news to Jamie and it wasn't going to be easy.

Twenty-Six

Consciousness came slowly at first, her body in no rush to wake up. As she became more awake, memories started filtering through until finally she remembered the car crash and she awoke fully. Groaning, she opened her eyes and realized that she was lying on her back looking up the strangest ceiling she'd ever seen, one made of dirt. *Daniel!* She sat up quickly, too quickly, and the room started to spin out of focus. Closing her eyes again, she took several deep breaths until the spinning stopped. Carefully she opened them again, thankful that the room didn't spin this time. It was very dark, with only a faint glow coming from the end of the room farthest from her, and it took a while for her eyes to adjust. When they did, what she saw made her gasp.

She was in a cell, a cage really. The wall behind her and the one to her left where made of dirt, but in front of her and to her right, metal bars joined the floor to the ceiling. Standing up gingerly, unsteady on her feet, she walked to the bars at the front of her cell. In the dark, she could make out that several of the bars formed a door but that they were held closed by a padlock on a chain. Even before she took them in her hand and shook them she knew they'd be locked, but she tried anyway. The door shook but did not give way.

"Kat!" The sound of his voice made her spin round. A face was pressed to the bars that ran between her cell and the next. She felt the relief rush through her as she went to him. "Daniel! Oh, honey, thank God you're okay." The words caught in her throat as she got near him and saw the bruises that marked the left side of his face. "Dear God, what did they do to you?"

He just shrugged. "I'm okay."

She reached up and gently ran a thumb over the side of his face, tears streaming down hers. "I'll get us out of this, honey, I promise."

Daniel just smiled sadly. "Thank you for trying to help me."

"It's not over yet so don't you dare give up on me, okay?" She tried to sound positive. "Finn and Jamie will be looking for us and they'll find us."

A groan from somewhere in the darkness made her jump. "What's that?"

"It's one of the others."

"The others that you told us about?"

She saw him nod.

Dear God, where were they? Well, she wasn't about to just sit around and wait for whoever had taken them to come back. She needed to try and figure out a way to get out of here, and fast.

"Is everybody down here locked in?" She couldn't see the rest of the room in the darkness. She could only just make out her own cell.

"Yes, all the time."

"Is there anyone else in there with you, Daniel? Anyone who can help us?"

He shook his head. "No, the boss keeps us all separate."

Not that she knew how that would help anyway, but if they were all separated in different cells and they were all padlocked in, as she was, then there was no hope of getting them all out. *You just need to get yourself out and get help.*

"Daniel, can you tell me about this room? Tell me everything you remember."

Her heart fell as she listened. There really was no way out. Their lives depended on Finn now.

Twenty-Seven

The men he'd sent to recover the boy stood silently in front of him as he paced back and forth angrily in his living room. Throwing the cigarette he was smoking into the empty fireplace behind him, he turned to them again. "What the hell were you thinking? You were supposed to get the boy, no one else."

"She recognized me, boss. I couldn't just leave her there."

"How did she recognize you? She doesn't know you."

The man visibly squirmed "Well, I sorta met her in town last week, in the coffee shop."

The boss got closer to him and stood mere inches from him before hissing into his face, "What do you mean you met her in the coffee shop? The rules are you never, ever, go into town. Are you telling me you broke those rules?"

The man nodded, not looking up to meet the boss's eyes. "I was driving through town and I needed the bathroom so I stopped."

There was no warning as the boss struck out, hitting the man across the side of the face with the back of his hand and sending him stumbling to his knees. "You couldn't use the side of the road like anyone else?" he shouted, covering the man in spittle. "Get him out of my sight. Now," he shouted to one of the other two men. He would decide what to do with him later. For now, he had to worry about the woman. He couldn't let her go; it was too late for that. "Clay, not you. I want you to go and get the woman and bring her to me."

He lit another cigarette and walked over to the window that looked out across his farm. It was a real working farm and how he made his legitimate income now that he was retired and his parents were long gone. He'd grown up here and although he'd worked in town for years, it was always assumed that when his folks got too old to look after it, he would. And so he had.

They hadn't known about his external interests, and it hadn't been until they were gone that he'd been able to become more than just a spectator. He'd spent years converting the farm, making it perfect for his needs, and in the process becoming one of the biggest players on the scene. He was not about to lose it all without a fight.

"Get your hands off me!" He heard her scream before he saw her as she was dragged down the corridor and pushed into the living room.

"You bitch!" Clay shouted as he hobbled into the room after her limping.

The boss laughed. "You're a feisty thing, aren't you? Haven't changed a bit."

He watched as she went completely still, searching his face before recognition slowly dawned. "You!"

"It's been a long time, Kat McKay. How have you been?"

"I don't believe this. You bastard!" She tried to lunge at him but Clay grabbed her around the waist before she could reach him.

"I am sorry about this. You weren't supposed to get caught up in it. It was only the boy I was after."

"That's supposed to make it better?"

"No, I don't suppose it does." He waved at Clay to let her go. "But you're here now and what happens next is up to you."

"What do you mean?"

The ringing of his phone interrupted them and, turning his back on her, he took the call.

"What news?" He listened for a moment. "Good to know. Phone me as soon as you hear anything else." Terminating the call, he turned back to Kat.

"Where were we?"

"Why are you doing this?"

"You wouldn't understand." He smiled. "I would say I enjoy it but that's only part of it. It makes me a hell of a lot of money, too."

"You enjoy hurting kids?" She was still in shock. "But you used to *teach* them!"

"One doesn't exclude the other," he said, laughing. "Besides, there's a lot more to it than that. It's a sport. You wouldn't believe how many of us there are."

She felt sick listening to him.

"I'm just one chapter. There are many more spread across the country. Hundreds of kids."

"A sport?" she made herself ask. The longer she kept him talking and the more details she learned, the better chance she'd have of figuring out a way to get out of here.

"Well, yes. There's horse racing, football, NASCAR. This is no different, really. If you have a winning fighter there's a fortune to be made."

Kat couldn't believe that this man, this man who had taught her in high school, was this monster. He'd been one of her favorite teachers; actually he was a firm favorite with most students, with his friendly manner and interesting lessons. She couldn't believe that all the while this monster had been hiding within him.

"Anyway, enough about that. I don't expect you to understand." He stepped toward her menacingly. "I do expect you to tell me everything you know, though."

"Tell you what, exactly? There's nothing to tell."

"What do the police know? How much did the boy tell them?"

"He doesn't know anything to tell them. You should know that. He's a kid. A scared kid. Why couldn't you just leave him alone?"

"I couldn't run the risk that he knew anything that would lead the police to me. That's why you need to tell me exactly what he told them."

"You honestly think I'm going to help you? Go to hell," she hissed.

The boss nodded to Clay. "Go and get the boy. I'm sure he'll help us make her talk."

"No!" Kat cried out. "Leave him alone!"

"Then you need to tell me everything they know."

There wasn't much to tell but she told him, every last thing she could think of, holding nothing back.

"There, that wasn't so hard, was it?"

"What's going to happen to us now?"

"You'll find out soon enough," he replied before telling Clay to take her back to her cell.

He was pleased. What Kat had told him confirmed the information his source had given him. They had no idea about him or the farm. He would just give it a bit of time for all the initial activity to die down and then he would get rid of her. It was one thing keeping a group of kids prisoner, but he didn't want to keep an adult captive. Especially one as smart as Kat. He remembered her from high school, and she'd been one of his brightest students. He wasn't about to risk that she could somehow escape. No, far better that the threat she posed be terminated once and for all and she could then be disposed of in the same place all the bodies had been disposed of over the years. One of the benefits of having a large farm; there were plenty of fields.

Twenty-Eight

"Do you think this has anything to do with what happened to Daniel?"

Finn was sitting on the couch in the living room at Jamie's house. He'd come here straight from where they'd found Kat's car to deliver the news.

"I don't know Jamie, it's too early to say at this stage but I'll be honest, I'll be very surprised if it's not."

Jamie nodded. "Of course it's connected. You know that as well as I do. What else could have happened?"

Finn just looked at her. She was right and he knew it.

"So they were just coming from the therapist's office?"

"It was Daniel's first session today. They had to have been on their way back."

"It can't have been blind luck that whoever took them knew they'd been on that road. They must have been watching them." This realization made Finn question his judgment. *Should I have given them some kind of protection?* He quickly shook this thought off, though. There had been no way of knowing that this would happen If he started down the road of self-blame he would lose focus and he couldn't afford to do that right now.

"Have you seen anything unusual, Jamie? Any cars hanging around?"

She shook her head. "No, nothing at all. And I would have noticed. It's not like we're on a main street out here. Any unusual cars would have stuck out like a sore thumb."

Finn nodded his head in agreement. She was right.

"We need to get hold of the CCTV from the therapist's office. If that was the last place we can definitely place them, then chances are fairly good that whoever took them was there, too. There would have been no other reason for Kat to be on that road, so they must have followed her there."

"Finn, you have to find her. I can't lose her. She's all I've got."

"Jamie, I promise you I'll find her." And he would; he just wished he could promise that he would find her alive.

***

Without the chief, the responsibility was weighing heavily on his shoulders. It's wasn't that he didn't know what needed doing; it was more that he just wanted to be out there doing it rather than directing things, which is what he was doing now. As the last place they were known to have visited was the next town over, he'd reached out to his counterpart there. As a bigger town, he'd been able to spare some of his own men to assist in the search as well as agreeing to take on the task of getting hold of the office staff from the therapist's office and get hold of a copy of the CCTV. As soon as they had it, they were going to bring it over to him.

He looked around at all the faces looking at him and was pleased to see that they all looked as concerned as he felt. "Okay, this is where we're at. CSI is processing the scene and will be recovering the vehicle. They'll contact us immediately if they find anything that could help us. For now, though, all we know is that Kat and Daniel were traveling back from a visit to Daniel's therapist's office and were in a car wreck and have vanished. We have to assume it was deliberate from the damage to the car and the paint found.

"We also have to assume it has something to do with Daniel's original abductors." He paused to look down at his notes. "We have no leads on them at all. What we do know is that this wasn't a case of a single child abduction. From what Daniel was able to tell us there were several more kids held with him and those kids were still alive when he last saw them."

He'd made copies of the photos of all the boys that Daniel had identified and now he handed them round. "These photos are how the kids looked when they were taken, but some are quite old now." He didn't know if it would be of any use but just having the photos would make them all realize what was at stake.

"I want all of you out there knocking on doors. Unfortunately, Daniel couldn't tell us where he had come from or how long he'd been out there, but we do know it had to have been close because he couldn't have gotten far in the state he was in. I don't care if you wake people up, or if these are people that you've known all your lives. Poke around, check outbuildings and, if they'll let you, go in and check houses." He stood up from where he'd been sitting on the corner of a desk

"Okay, that's it folks. Get out there, keep in touch and report back anything you think is out of the ordinary. Anything at all."

The sounds of chairs being pushed back and the murmur of conversation followed him as he walked into the chief's office before closing the door behind him and shutting it all out. It felt strange sitting in the Chief's chair but he needed the quiet to think, to make sure he wasn't missing anything.

Quiet wasn't what he got, though, as the phone in his pocket started ringing, the sound very loud in the silence of the room. Pulling it out, he saw that it was Sally. *Damn!* He'd left her cleaning up and with a promise that he would call her and let her know what was happening. That had been hours ago. Sheepishly, he picked up. "Hey."

"Hey, you. Everything okay? I've been worried."

He sighed. "I'm sorry. I know I promised to call but things sorta got out of hand here."

"Oh no!" He could hear the concern in her voice. "Nothing serious, I hope?"

"Actually, yeah." He filled her in on what had happened, trying not to sound as worried as he felt. She was bound to be affected; she'd grown attached to Daniel, too.

"Oh, that poor boy! And Kat! Can I do anything?"

"No, there's nothing you can do. But I'm not going to make it back tonight, I don't think. I'm sorry."

"Don't be silly. No apology necessary. You need to find them. Do you want me to stay?"

He didn't. And it wasn't because he had no idea when he'd get back, it was because all he could think about was how he would feel if he lost Kat. "No, better not. I have no idea when I'll be back or how long for. I'll give you a call when I have any news, okay?"

"That's fine. Take care and bring them home, okay?"

"I'll try."

He ended the call and sat for a moment looking at the now silent phone, frustrated with himself. He could try and kid himself that the only reason he couldn't stop thinking about Kat was because she was missing, but he would be lying to himself. He hadn't stopped thinking about her since she'd first come back to town. Yeah, he didn't know if he could forgive her, but that didn't stop the way he *felt*. Now was not the time for such thoughts, though; he had to find them before it was too late.

He thought everyone had gone when he came out of the office and he was surprised to find Deputy Carver still hadn't left. He had his back to him and he could see he was on his cell phone, talking animatedly. Deliberately closing the office door hard, he watched as he quickly put the cell phone away. "Sorry boss, had to make a quick call."

Finn resolved to have another talk to the chief about this kid when he was well enough.

"And it was so important that you had to make it now rather than get out there and do the job you're paid to do?"

He could see that he wanted to make some sort of sarcastic retort, but the look on Finn's face must have been enough to tell him that it wasn't a good idea and he kept his mouth shut. "No? Well, get out there then. You're no use to me sitting around here."

***

The deputy from Charlton charged with obtaining the CCTV had finally arrived and he and Finn were both sitting in front of the TV in the main squad room.

"Thanks for getting it so fast," Finn said to the deputy as he took the disk out of his bag.

"No problem, though the woman I dragged out of bed to let us in to get it probably wouldn't agree."

Thankfully, the chief had invested some of the budget last year in getting them an up-to-date media set-up that would allow them to review the footage. Precious hours, or even days, could have been lost if they'd had to get someone else to do it for them. Putting the disk in, they selected the timeframe when Kat and Daniel had been due to arrive and, sure enough, there they were. They watched as Kat parked her car in the lot and they walked across the asphalt to the main doors to the center where the therapist was located.

It was odd watching them like this, their movements jilted and puppet like on the feed. The center had several cameras, but Finn was only interested in the one pointing at the car lot, deducing that if they had been followed they would have been unlikely to have been followed actually inside the building.

"Okay, now slow it down," he told the deputy.

"What are we looking for?"

Finn sighed. "I don't know. Anything that looks out of place, anyone acting strangely. I'll guess we'll know it when we see it."

***

It was a cup of coffee and a severe case of eye strain later that he finally spotted it. It wasn't what was there; it was what wasn't there. They were just watching the tape of Kat and Daniel leaving when it hit him.

"There!" He pointed at the top right hand corner of the screen. The front half of a red pick-up was just visible reversing out of a parking spot, just after Kat's car had left the lot.

"What about it?" The deputy looked confused.

"Go back to when Kat and Daniel arrived." He was right; he just knew it.

Playing the footage back again from the moment they arrived, they watched that corner of the screen and not long after Kat parked her car, the red pick-up arrived.

"I'm sorry, but I don't see what's so special about it. There are lots of red cars in the lot coming and going throughout the tape."

"I know that," Finn said impatiently, "but keep your eyes on that one and keep watching it until Kat comes out again."

They watched the tape again in silence. "Do you see now?" The deputy shook his head. "Look at it. You can only see the front half of the vehicle but you can see the cab. From the moment it arrives until the moment it leaves again, do you see anyone getting out of it?"

He could almost see the light go on in the deputy's head. "No, because no one did!"

"Exactly. Now why would you drive into a parking lot and just sit in your truck for an hour and then leave again?"

"You wouldn't."

"That's them." Finned jabbed his finger at the screen. "That's who ran them off the road."

"Okay, but now what?" The deputy leaned forward and squinted at the screen. "There's no way of making out the license. The angle is wrong. It's pointing away from us."

Finn's heart sank. He was right; even with enhancement they wouldn't be able to see the plate as it simply hadn't been captured.

Finn's hand slamming down on the desk made the deputy jump. "Damnit! Why is nothing going our way?"

"But who's saying this is the first time they followed her, though?"

Finn stilled. *He was right! Why hadn't he thought of that?* He clapped his hand on the deputy's shoulder. "Good point. If he was caught there he may well have been caught somewhere else, somewhere where we can see the license plate." He thought for a moment. "He hasn't been out of the hospital long and I know that Kat has only been into town a couple of times since he has." *Good news for us for a change,* Finn thought. "I'll give Jamie McKay a call and find out if she can help us narrow down our search window. Then we can contact anyone in town with CCTV and see if they've caught anything."

Feeling energized, he went to his office and called Jamie. As he suspected, Kat had only been into town twice since Daniel had come out of the hospital, as far as Jamie was aware. One of those visits was just yesterday when she'd come to collect the property records. "We'll start with her visit yesterday as it was the nearest in time to the actual attack. There were two places she visited yesterday, apart from here: the council offices and the coffee shop," he instructed the deputy. "You go to the council offices and get their footage and

I'll go and grab the coffee shops'. Get back here as quickly as you can."

"Will they be open now?" The deputy checked his watch "It's only five a.m."

Finn realized with a start that he had completely lost track of time. "No, they won't. You're right. The diner opens at six, though, so I'll head over there as soon as it opens. We'll have to wait until a bit later for the other footage."

He was waiting at the glass doors of the diner when it opened promptly at six. He didn't want to get his hopes up; he wasn't even sure they had CCTV.

"Hey, Jen, you got a minute?" Jen had been behind the counter here for as long as he could remember and used to serve him milkshakes when he was a kid. A large, kindly gray-haired lady, you didn't talk to her if you were in a hurry as she was very difficult to stop once she got started.

"For you, honey, always."

"Do you have CCTV here?" He looked around and saw a camera in the corner of the room and pointed at it. "Is that a real camera or a dummy?"

"It's real. We got it after that robbery a couple of summers back." She put a cup in front of him and started to pour him a coffee from a glass jug that seemed permanently attached to her hand. "Do you remember that summer? That would have been when..."

He held up his hand. "Sorry, Jen, I really can't talk right now. I need to get a copy of your footage from yesterday and it's really urgent."

She didn't seem in the slightest offended. "Sure, come through the back and I'll get it for you."

Leaving her with promises that he would return soon to catch up, he took the footage and hurried back to the station. The deputy was already there and watching the footage he had gotten from the council offices.

"Anything?" Finn asked, coming to stand behind him.

"Not so far."

They both watched silently as the images played across the screen until they got to the point where Kat and Daniel arrived. Despite going over it slowly, it was clear that the camera hadn't caught anything.

"Fingers crossed we have more luck with this one." Finn handed the disk in his hand to the deputy and watched as he replaced the one currently in the machine and pressed play. Immediately, the image came on screen Finn's heart fell. The camera covered the interior of the coffee shop, as he'd expected, but you could only see a small section of the road outside the diner. He had hoped that it would be at a better angle. *Damn!*

He watched as Kat appeared on the screen and collided with a man he didn't recognize who was just coming out of the bathroom. He didn't seem pleased and he didn't need to be able to lip read to see that he said something angrily to her before leaving.

"Looks like he's getting into a red car, or truck," the deputy said, pointing to an area at the top of the screen. He was right; you could just make out the bottom half of a red vehicle. "It's no good to us, though. We can't see enough." As they watched, though, the car pulled forward and reversed towards the shop window to make a u-turn. As it did, for a brief moment, the license was in full view.

Not believing his luck, Finn quickly grabbed a pencil from a holder on the desk and a piece of paper and jotted the number down. Going to the nearest computer and switching it on, he ran it through the database. And was immediately disappointed. The vehicle was shown as belonging to Mark Flint. The man on the footage must have been one of his farm hands. Finn had known Flint for years, since he had taught him in high school, and he knew without a doubt that he wasn't involved in this in any way. He didn't know the farm hand, though, so it was worth a drive out there even if it was just to eliminate them.

"Have you got time to come out with me to the farm or do you need to get back to Carlton?"

"My boss said I'm to give you whatever help you need so sure, why not?"

***

"What's your first name, kid?" Finn asked the deputy as they drove up to the farm.

"John."

"Well, John, thanks for all your help back there."

"No problem. Good change from issuing parking tickets in Carlton."

"Here we are. This is the Flint farm," Finn told him, pointing to a dirt road after they'd been driving for twenty minutes. "It's about two miles up this road."

The road was full of bumps and potholes and by the time they arrived Finn felt like they'd been put through a tumble drier.

Getting out of the cruiser, they climbed the steps to the front porch and knocked on the door.

"Finn! Gosh, how long's it been?" The door was opened by a man who bore an uncanny resemblance to Colonel Sanders.

"Hi, Mark." Finn shook his extended hand. "How have you been doing?"

"I'm very well. To what do I owe the pleasure of your visit?"

Finn described the man seen on the surveillance footage and explained that they needed to speak to him but he stopped short of telling him why.

"Ah, that sounds like Kenny. Not the most sociable or friendly of people but he's a good worker."

"Any chance we could have a quick word with him?"

Flint shook his head. "I'm sorry, Finn, he's not here. I've sent him on an errand and he won't be back until tomorrow."

"Can you get a hold of him and ask him to come back early?"

"I've got no way of getting a hold of him. He doesn't have a cell. I really am sorry, Finn. I'd help if I could."

"What about the truck. Is that here?"

"He's got it with him, I'm afraid."

Disappointed, Finn told Flint that he would be back tomorrow and they returned to the cruiser.

"Didn't that seem a little odd to you?" John asked as they pulled out of the yard.

"What?"

"Who doesn't have a cell phone these days?"

"Unfortunately, out here a lot of people don't have them. The service is awful and a lot of the farm hands wouldn't know what to do with one."

Twenty-Nine

You pay peanuts and you get monkeys, wasn't that how the saying went? Well, he sure seemed to employ a bunch of monkeys. "Why didn't you warn me they were on their way here?" he shouted into the phone.

"I didn't know."

"I told you I wanted to know everything that was going on in the investigation. You've let me down."

He had no choice now; he had to run, and fast. Shouting orders to his men, he told them to put their escape plan into action. He'd had one for years, always knowing that this day could possibly come but never actually believing it would.

He didn't care about the farm itself. He was not into all that sentimental clap trap, but it did represent a sizeable chunk of money. *Oh well,* he thought, *there was plenty more where that came from.* Going to his safe, hidden behind a picture in his dining room, he took out two large briefcases filled with cash. On top of them was a worn black book. The book contained all the details of the others like him and was invaluable. Putting the book inside his jacket, he looked around. There was so much here that he should dispose of but he just didn't have time. No matter; there was nothing he could do to hide it any more. He grabbed the cases and stepped outside.

"The trucks are all loaded," Clay told him, coming out from the nearest barn. "What do you want us to do with the woman?" He thought about it for a moment. He hadn't had time to deal with her yet and he didn't want to take her with them.

"Leave her and the boy behind." It was because of them that all this had happened. He would leave them where they wouldn't be found and when they were, it would be too late. The thought of the death that awaited them made him smile.

"Yes, boss," Clay replied before trotting back over to the barn.

***

Something was going on. "What's happening?" Kat tried to get an answer from the men who were roughly removing the other boys from their cells. "Where are you taking them?" But they just ignored her. Gripping the bars of her cell, she screamed at them. "Leave them alone!" But they took no notice. The boys were mostly silent, doing as they were told and following the men meekly. She expected them to come for her and for Daniel, but as one after the other of the boys was removed and no one approached their cells she started to fear the worst. As the last boy was led out, the room was suddenly plunged into complete darkness as the light was switched off, the only light now coming from the still open door.

"Wait! Come back! You can't just leave us here!" she screamed at the top of her lungs, but to no avail. Despairingly, she watched as the light from the door finally disappeared as it was closed with a resounding clank.

Her own breathing was heavy in her ears in the silence that followed. Feeling her way, she went to the bars that separated her cell from Daniel's. She could hear him sniffling in the darkness and called out to him.

"Daniel, honey, it's okay." She heard him move closer to her and felt his hand reach for her through the bars. "We'll get out of here, I promise." She was confused. Where had they all gone? "Daniel, has this ever happened before, where they've taken you all out at the same time?"

"No, they only ever take the ones that are fighting," he whispered, the tremble in his voice giving away how much this worried him.

"Okay. I know it's hard, but try not to worry. I'm sure they'll be back soon." Though she was trying to convince Daniel, she didn't believe it for a second herself. Something had happened, something that was making them run, and she clung to the hope that the police were getting close. She'd not given a thought to oxygen before, as the constantly opening and closing door from the room that was linked to the outside replenished their supply. But now, without that, how long did they have? She didn't know but she did know that the police had better hurry. If it wasn't the lack of oxygen, it would be the lack of water that killed them. Either way, she knew for certain that one of them would.

Thirty

He'd hoped to have some news for her by now but he had nothing. As Finn followed Jamie into her kitchen and faced her, he could tell she hadn't slept. Her eyes were swollen from crying and they were ringed with dark circles.

"I'm sorry, Jamie. We're doing everything we can but there's no sign of them yet."

"You must have something to go on!"

"We've had a couple of leads from some surveillance footage that we're following up, but so far we've drawn a blank."

"Well, they can't have just vanished. They've got to be out there somewhere." Tears were spilling out of her eyes now.

"And I promise you, I won't rest until we find them." And he wouldn't. They were doing everything they could at the moment, though. The whole department was out there, searching. The surveillance footage had all been checked now and the only leads were the ones they'd found on the footage from the therapist's office and the coffee shop. Until he could go back and speak to the farm hand tomorrow, that was a dead end, too. They were still waiting for the forensic report but that was going to take some time. The analysis of the paint had to be sent out to a specialist lab, one that took cases from all over the state, so it would be several days before they got any news on that front.

Leaving her with a promise that he would get in touch the minute he had any news, he drove back into town. John had waited in the car while he spoke to Jamie and, once they'd parked the car back at the station, he told him to go home and come back first thing in the morning. He'd already cleared it with his boss that he could use him for another day and though it was only mid-afternoon, he'd been up all night and needed some rest.

He wasn't heading home yet, though. As he walked into the station, Sandy handed him a big envelope. "This got delivered when you were out." Momentarily confused, he suddenly remembered. *The missing boys' case files.* Taking them into to the chief's office, he opened the envelope and slid them out.

The next few hours were spent examining them for anything that connected the two cases or anything that connected them to Daniel's case, but he couldn't find anything. The combination of spending the night before staring at surveillance footage and the hours spent combing over the files had given him a terrible headache, and when he saw that the night shift deputies had arrived he decided to call it a day. Tomorrow they would go back to Flint's farm and speak to the farm hand and maybe, just maybe, something would break.

Thirty-One

As Finn drove his cruiser onto the farm, he was struck by the silence. When they'd been up here yesterday, the yard had been a flurry of activity as it was a working farm. This time, though, there was no movement. Pulling up outside the main farmhouse, Finn and the deputy from Carlton stepped out of the car and looked around.

"Quiet here." John said exactly what Finn was thinking.

"Yeah, too quiet."

Walking up the steps to the porch, Finn knocked on the door and waited. Hearing no movement inside, he looked through the window to the left of the front door. Through a gap in the drapes he saw that everything looked normal. "Strange. Let's go and take a look in the barn."

Finn was getting worried now. What if the farm hand did have something to do with this? What if he'd found out they were looking for him and he'd harmed Mr. Flint?

As they approached, they could see tire tracks in the mud that ended at the barn doors. "Let's get this open." With John's help, he lifted the heavy metal bar and pulled the door open. They walked in and paused, taking a few seconds to allow their eyes to become accustomed to the gloom. It soon became apparent that the barn was empty, though from the tracks on the ground it was clear that it hadn't always been.

"These tracks look recent to me," John said, crouching down to take a closer look.

Finn nodded. "Agreed. It doesn't help us, though." He looked around. "Something is very wrong here. Have you ever seen a farm this quiet?"

"Can't say that I have."

"I think we need to get into that house. I think we've enough to justify it without a warrant. For all we know, Flint could be laying in there right now, injured."

"You're the boss," John replied, standing up. As he did, he disturbed some of the hay and other detritus that lay on the barn floor and something glinted, catching Finn's eye. "What was that?"

"What was what?"

But Finn didn't reply, bending down and pushing the dirt aside with his finger. There, lying in the mud, was a gold stud earring. "Quick, go and grab an evidence bag from the cruiser." He'd need to show Jamie to be sure, but it looked just like the studs that Kat wore.

As he waited for John to return, he stood up and with his foot started clearing the area around the earring to see if there was anything else lying there hidden. He had cleared a good-sized area by the time the deputy returned and he was just about to stop when he felt the surface underneath his shoe change. Immediately intrigued, he noticed that part of the floor appeared to be made out of wooden planks.

"Come here and give me a hand with this," he called over to John and they both knelt and started clearing the area by hand. It quickly became clear that what they were looking at was some kind of hatch, locked from the outside.

"Damn, it's locked," Finn said as he rattled the now visible padlock.

"We could go into town and get some tools and come back later," the deputy suggested.

"No, that will take too long." Finn looked around the barn. "It's a farm. There must be an axe or something we could use to smash the wood around here somewhere."

Going in different directions, they checked the rest of the barn.

"Over here. I've got one!" Finn looked over to where John held up a large axe.

"Great, let's get that hatch open."

Finn realized he was holding his breath as he watched John bring the axe down on the hatch. It splintered with the first blow and the second separated it from the metal padlock. Having no idea what they would find, they both drew their weapons before Finn carefully reached down and lifted the hatch. Taking his flashlight from his belt, he aimed the beam down the hole. As nothing came flying up to meet them and take their heads off, he risked leaning over and looking down, following the beam of light.

Secured into the fairly narrow square shaft was a metal ladder which, from what he could see, dropped about twenty feet before meeting the ground. "How are you with small enclosed spaces?" he asked wryly. He wasn't about to admit it himself, but it was one of the few things that actually bothered him and looking down the hole, he could feel himself start to sweat.

"You okay, boss?"

He must have looked worried because John was looking at him as if he was about to faint. "I'm fine." He gestured toward the hole with his gun. "After you."

Keeping his gun aimed down the hole, he watched as the deputy tested the first rung of the ladder before, satisfied that it would hold his weight, he gingerly made his way down. Once at the bottom, he disappeared from sight briefly before Finn heard him shout excitedly. "Boss! Get down here, you need to see this!"

Taking a deep breath, he stepped on to the first rung. *Here goes,* he thought as he lowered himself down, the light from above becoming dimmer and dimmer the further down he went. Once at the bottom, he noticed a door that hadn't been visible from above which now stood open, spilling a faint light at the bottom of the shaft. Going through it, he saw what had gotten John so excited.

The room took his breath away. Partly because it was so unexpected, but also because of its sheer size. It was huge. It was an amazing feat of engineering, carved as it was out of the ground, and must have been a long time in the execution. There were supporting pillars at regular intervals except at the very center of the room where there was a clearly marked boxing ring, around which was seating for approximately fifty people. On the far side of the room was another door; this one, though, was locked from the outside. Skirting the ring to get to it, Finn was pleased to see that this one was also made of wood.

"We'll need the axe again." Looking around as he waited for the deputy to return with it, details that he'd missed on first glance were now jumping out at him. The floor of the ring was covered in dark, coppery stains that could only be blood and the floor was scattered with bits of paper. Dropping down to one knee, he picked on up. It was what was left of a betting slip. Finn felt sick to his stomach thinking about what must have gone on in this room. It was one thing hearing Daniel describe it; it was quite another to stand in the room where it all happened.

***

The smell hit him first as he opened the door. A wave of stale air swept out of the room as he let the fresh air in and on it was carried the stench of unwashed bodies and what could only be described as sewage. It was pitch black behind the door but his flashlight soon revealed a cord dangling from the ceiling. Pulling on it, a single bulb swinging from a wire lit up, casting a faint glow.

The sight of the rows of empty cages shocked him and his feet felt as though there were rooted to the spot. A noise to his left made him jump and he quickly swung round, holding his gun out in front of him. "Stop! Police!" he shouted, his voice echoing around the cavernous room.

"Finn? Finn! It's me, Kat! Over here!"

The voice sounded like it came from the far end of the room and Finn and the deputy, who had followed him, quickly dashed over. They found them in the last two cells on the left hand side and Finn couldn't help but flinch when he saw them. Both were filthy, their clothes torn, and a terrible smell was coming from buckets in the corners of the cells.

"Go topside and call an ambulance. Tell them to put their foot down. See if any of the other cruisers have any bolt-cutters and tell them to get here, too," he told the deputy as he looked at the metal bars and locks. "We're not going to be able to get these open with the axe."

"Are you hurt?" He turned his attention back to Kat and Daniel.

"No, not hurt. Just very thirsty and hungry," she replied, her voice raspy from lack of water. "Thank God you found us."

"Don't worry, we'll get you out of here soon." He looked around the room again, taking it all in. "Have you been down here since you were snatched?"

Kat nodded. "Yes. But Finn, there were others, kids. I don't know how many. They came and took them all and never came back."

***

Finn stood back and watched as the paramedics and deputies helped them climb the ladder and out of their underground hell. They were both weak, dehydrated and hungry and had to be helped into the back of the waiting ambulance. Three other cruisers were parked just outside the barn now along with the ambulance, and he could see the shock on his men's faces. None of them had ever come across anything like this before. Once Kat and Daniel had been safely put in the ambulance, he gestured for his deputies to gather around him.

"No one is to go downstairs until CSI says it's okay to do so, but we need to find out where this bastard has gone so I want the house turned upside down. Rip up floors if you have to, but give me something."

As they left to follow his orders, he pulled his cell phone from his pocket.

"Hey, it's me."

"Hi there," Sally replied.

"Look, are you at work?"

"Yep, in the middle of a twelve-hour shift. Did you want to get together? I can take a break if you want to meet me in the canteen later."

"I'm sorry, Sally, I can't. I've actually called to give you the head's up." He briefly filled her in. "Could you make sure you get security to stay with them when they arrive? I don't think they'll try and snatch them again but I haven't got a deputy to spare at the moment to come over there with them."

"Sure I will, and I'll make sure I'm there when they arrive. It might make them feel better to see a friendly face."

"Thank you, I'm sure it will. After this is all done, I promise we'll get together and catch up." As he put the phone down, he felt lucky. There weren't many women who would put up with the hours he put in in his job and the fact that he couldn't ever make plans. It was about time he started appreciating her a bit more. Walking over to the ambulance which was packing up to leave, he popped his head inside. From the expression on Kat's face, she was none too impressed to be strapped to a gurney. "Hey guys, Sally is going to meet you at the hospital."

"I don't need to go to the hospital, Finn. I'm perfectly fine." She frowned at him. "I want to help you catch this guy. Deputize me, give me a gun and let's go nail the bastard."

Finn shook his head. "Not a chance. We've got it covered."

"We need to go now, sir," the paramedic said, appearing beside him to shut the doors.

"I'll call Jamie and let her know what's happened," he said, stepping back to let them close the doors.

Thirty-Two

It felt like he hadn't had any sleep for days and his eyes felt gritty as he pulled his hands down across his face. *I need a shave, too,* he thought as his stubble scratched at his hands. He didn't have time to worry about that right now, though. Despite bringing Kat and Daniel home safely, there was no time to celebrate. The monster was on the run and they needed to track him down before he had time to go underground again.

It had been a shock for the whole department when they'd discovered who had been responsible, most of them having known Mark Flint at some point in their lives, and it was almost as if they felt even more determined to bring him to justice now, as if he'd wronged them personally.

He had a meeting scheduled in a couple of hours with them all to once again go over what they knew so far, and to establish the next course of action. The problem was, he didn't know what the next course of action should be. Whether it was because he was too tired, or too personally involved, he just couldn't seem to think straight. This case was getting more complicated by the day and, he admitted to himself, he was out of his depth.

Grabbing his jacket from the back of the chair where he was sat in the chief's office, he slipped it on. He had a couple of hours before he needed to be back. Time to go and speak to the one person whose advice he trusted.

The chief lived in a house in town, about ten minutes' walk from the police station. While most people chose to live on the outside of town where the houses were larger, the chief had always told Finn that with his job he wanted to be close so he could get to the station in minutes if he needed to. The storms of the previous days had cleared and the sun was shining so he decided to walk the short distance rather than take the car.

As he pressed the doorbell, he wondered if he should have called ahead. The chief had only just been released from the hospital and the last thing Finn wanted to do was disturb his rest. He needn't have worried though. As his wife ushered him into the living room, he could see that the chief was pleased to see him.

"How are you feeling?"

"Bored." The chief rose to shake his hand. "Please tell me you've come with some interesting news. The warden," he indicated the kitchen where his wife was making coffee, "has banned me from getting over-excited so I'm limited to watching daytime TV and a bit of gentle gardening."

"Well, I've come for your advice, actually." Finn spent the next few minutes filling him in on everything that had happened since he had been taken in to the hospital and where they now stood in the investigation. "So that's where we're at right now. And, to be honest, I'm not sure where to go next." It felt good to share the load with his boss and he felt a bit of the tension leave his shoulders.

"You've done everything I would have done, so don't beat yourself up. I still can't believe this has been going on under our noses all these years." He shook his head. "But you're right. I think this is too big for the department now, Finn. We just don't have the resources. And besides, there's no telling if he's even still in the state."

"You think I should call in the Feds, don't you."

"I think you have to. They should have been called in earlier and I take full responsibility for that, but if you don't call them in now there are going to be a lot of questions if this turns out bad."

Finn knew he was right; he just needed to hear someone else say it. "So, when are you coming back to work?" he laughed. "Or are you going to wait until I've sorted this mess out before you do?"

"Well, we need to talk about that. But now is not the time. Once this is over, we'll have a chat."

"I don't like the sound of that. You are coming back, aren't you?" Finn could tell that he was keeping something from him.

The chief sighed "Well, I wanted to talk to you about this when you didn't have so much on your mind but no, I'm not coming back. I'm old, Finn, and this heart attack was a warning sign telling me it's time to hang up my badge."

"You've got to come back. The department won't be the same without you." Finn tried to make himself smile. "Besides, I don't want to have to train a new chief. It took me forever to get you just the way I like you."

The chief laughed. "Thanks! But no, I don't think you'll need to train a new chief. I think you should put yourself forward for the job."

Finn shook his head. "No. I've told you before I don't want the responsibility, and this case has reminded me why."

"Well, promise me you'll think about it? You've done a great job on this one, Finn, even if you don't think so and the town would be lucky to have you. And you know, with my backing, it's practically yours for the taking."

"I'll think about it but I'm not promising anything, okay? I'd better get back. I've got a phone call to make."

***

He felt somehow lighter as he made his way back to the station. The fresh air and sunshine had done him good, leaving him feeling invigorated. Settling behind his desk, he found the number for the local FBI field office in the chief's rolodex and made the call. He knew he should have called them earlier; anything involving a kidnapping was under their jurisdiction, but it wasn't a straightforward case. They wouldn't see it that way, though, he was sure, and he fully expected to have to explain himself.

He hadn't had many dealings with the FBI; Brecon Point was not exactly a hub of criminal activity. But they had crossed paths before and he couldn't say he was fond of them. The chief was right, though; they had access to resources he simply didn't and they needed all the help they could get. Surprisingly, the Special Agent In Charge was able to take his call immediately and, as expected, put him through the wringer for not calling them in sooner. Nevertheless, he promised to get an agent there as soon as he could, certainly by the end of the day.

The local field office was just over a hundred miles away so that gave him, at absolute minimum, a couple of hours before they arrived.

Thirty-Three

It was nearly six p.m. and his stomach was reminding him that he'd barely eaten all day. He was just considering whether to order take-out when there was a knock on the office door. Before he had chance to speak, it was opened and a man dressed in a suit walked in.

"It's customary to wait to be invited in when you knock on a door." It was out of his mouth before he could stop it. He was in no doubt that this was the agent sent by the field office. He had all the telling features of an FBI agent; the suit and tie, the closely cut hair and the arrogant expression which seemed to come with the badge.

"I'm Agent Callahan, FBI. Deputy Groves, I presume?" he asked, ignoring Finn's comment.

"Acting Chief Groves, yes."

Agent Callahan looked around the office. "This will do."

"I'm sorry? This will do for what?"

"I'll need an office to work."

Who did this guy think he was? "We have an interview room down the hall. You can use that."

Finn met and held the agent's eyes. He hadn't expected the pissing contest to start so soon, but he wasn't about to roll over and let this prick march in here and start acting like he was the hired help.

"That'll work," the agent finally said after a long pause.

"Can you bring everything you have on this case so far so I can get to work, please?"

"Well, I was just going to get some food and then I can go through it all with you."

The agent held up his hand. "Thanks, but no. I always go through everything on my own first. If you could make yourself available if I have any questions, that would be great."

And with that he turned and left the office, leaving Finn standing there.

Following him out of the office, he saw that Deputy Carver was at his desk doing paperwork. "Carver, get all the information on the case so far and take it in to Agent Callahan, will you? He'll be in the interview room." Deciding against the take-out, he told Carver that he would be back in an hour and to contact him if he was needed and left the building.

Thirty-Four

He'd grabbed Chinese food from the restaurant in town and had just settled down at his kitchen counter to eat it when his cell began to buzz on his belt. With a sigh, he put down his fork, his meal untouched, and checked the screen. It was work.

"Yes," he answered, probably sounding brusquer than he intended.

"I hope I'm not interrupting anything, but if it's not too much trouble would you mind coming back to the station?" The sarcasm in Agent Callahan's voice was obvious and it was all he could do not to rise to the bait.

"Of course, after I've had something to eat. Unless it's urgent, of course?" Finn said with an equal amount of sarcasm.

"No, take your time. We've only got a bunch of missing kids. I'm sure they can wait."

Finn glared at the phone as Callahan disconnected. He'd barely left the office at all for the past few days and this guy was implying he wasn't taking the case seriously. Taking a deep breath, he returned his attention to his food but found that after a couple of mouthfuls he'd lost his appetite. He put the cartons in the fridge, though he had no idea if he'd get back to eat them any time soon, and left.

***

"Ah, you decided to join us. Thank you." Finn ignored Callahan's sarcasm as he walked into the squad room, surprised to see the other deputies gathered there.

"Take a seat please. I was just about to start my briefing." Finn looked at the other deputies who all looked equally baffled.

"Right. Now that you're all here, let's get on with it." He looked around the room. "I'm Agent Callahan, FBI, and I'm here as this investigation is now a federal matter, as it should have been from the beginning." Finn smarted under the blatant criticism but held his tongue.

"I've gone over the case notes and I feel there are a couple of things that are worth revisiting." He looked down at his notes. "The first thing is the farmhouse. I want it searched again to make sure you haven't missed anything. If this has been going on for as long as this kid says it has, there has to be something there that could give us a lead. The second is the kid." He looked directly at Finn. "Are we sure that he's told us everything? Have we pushed him hard enough?"

"He's told us what he knows. All of it." There was no way Finn was letting this piece of work near Daniel if he could help it. The rest of the briefing was more of the same and by the end of it Finn was left in no doubt that Callahan thought his department was completely incompetent.

"Can I have a word?" Finn was trying very hard to control his temper.

"What about?" Callahan didn't even look at him, preferring to carry on gathering his papers together.

"In my office, not out here." Callahan didn't move. "Now, please."

Looking at him, Callahan smirked and raised an eyebrow. "Okay."

Finn closed the door gently before turning to face him. "How dare you."

"How dare I what?"

"How dare you walk in here and just take over the investigation like that without even discussing your plans with me first."

"I think you're mistaken. I don't have to discuss my plans with you first. This is now a federal investigation and, as such, I'm in charge."

"And you don't think it would have been a common courtesy to speak to me about it first?"

"I would have if you had been here. But you weren't. Besides, my priority is finding these kids, not treading on eggshells around you."

He was right, of course. Finn realized that. He would just have to put up with him for now. It didn't mean he had to like it, though, and he most definitely didn't like it.

Callahan checked his watch. "So, do you want to stay here and discuss it some more or shall we head out to the scene? My search team will be there by now and I don't want to leave them waiting."

***

He was still angry as they pulled up at the farmhouse to search it for a second time, but he was determined to keep a lid on it. "I don't know what you expect to find. We've searched the house already," he told Callahan after his car pulled up behind him and he stepped out.

"I'm well aware of that. But my team," he paused as he nodded to where a group of men were gathered around an unmarked van, "are specially trained and if there's anything to find, they'll find it."

Finn knew he was right. They couldn't afford to miss anything and his deputies were simply not trained for this sort of stuff.

"Who else have you invited to the party?" he asked as another van pulled up alongside the other one. "I've brought our own CSI team. Just in case we find anything."

Finn hated to admit it but he was impressed. He didn't have to like him but he did seem to be throwing a ton of resources at this.

Following the search team into the house, he watched as they methodically started their work. They were like a finely-tuned machine and each room was carefully examined with very little unnecessary chatter. They'd worked their way from the top of the house down and hadn't found anything by the time they'd reached the ground floor. They'd just started in the living room, though, when a ripple of excitement could be felt. He followed as Callahan stepped through the door.

"What have you found?" Callahan asked before Finn had chance to speak.

"This, boss."

They both watched as one of the search team pressed a panel that was concealed in the back of a bookcase set against the back wall. As he did, the whole panel slid sideways, revealing a staircase which descended underground. *Not again!* Finn groaned to himself at the thought of another small, dark place.

"I'm guessing you didn't know about this as it's not in your report?"

"You know full well I didn't," Finn snapped. "Try not to be so happy about it." Resisting the urge to wipe the condescending smirk of Callahan's face was getting harder by the minute.

"Go and let CSI know what we've found and that they're needed," he instructed one of the search team. "We don't have any time to waste on this so I suggest we limit it to just you and I down there until CSI have done their bit."

Great, just me and mouth almighty. What a treat. After Callahan had turned on a light by pressing a switch at the top of the descent, Finn gingerly followed him down the stairs which were made of wooden treads placed on steps carved out of dirt. There were only about a dozen to negotiate before the walls opened and they found themselves standing inside a room the size of a large office.

Unlike the fighting arena, there were no pillars holding up the ceiling here; it simply wasn't big enough. But what it lacked in size, it made up for in comfort. The floor of the room was almost entirely covered in a massive rug on which rested a huge, black leather couch. That wasn't what drew their attention, though. It was the enormous, flat screen TV hanging from the wall directly opposite it. To the right of the TV there was yet another bookcase, but unlike the one upstairs which had been filled with books, this one was filled with DVD's.

Pulling a pair of latex gloves from his pocket and slipping them on, Finn reached forward and pulled a DVD from one of the many stacks. It was just a disc in a clear plastic case. Turning it over in his hands, he found that there was writing on the reverse. A date. Pulling another one off the shelf, he checked that one, too. It was exactly the same, unmarked except for a date.

"We'd better take a look." Finn knew he wasn't going to like what he was about to see as Callahan took one of the discs from his hands and, removing it from its case, inserted it into a slot on the side of the TV. Finding the remote on the arm of the couch, Finn turned the TV on and they both stood and waited for the disc to load.

There was absolute silence in the room as the first disk started to play. Neither of them moved as they struggled to take in what they saw on the screen.

"Turn it off." Callahan told him.

For once, Finn agreed with him and he flicked the switch on the remote, returning the screen to blackness.

"I'll get a specialist team to go through the discs to see if we can identify any of the people who are on them."

Finn didn't envy them their task. He didn't think he could cope with having to sit through hours of watching them. Returning his attention to the room, he looked at the rug thoughtfully.

"Help me get this table out of the way," he called out to Callahan, waiting until he had grabbed it at one end. This guy clearly had a penchant for hiding things underground and Finn wanted to see if his hunch was right. Sure enough, once they'd moved the table out of the way and rolled back the rug, a floor safe was revealed.

"It's locked." Finn pulled uselessly at the handle.

"We'll get it transported back and our tech team will get it open."

There was nothing else for him to do down there so he made his way back upstairs to observe the rest of the search.

Thirty-Five

Everything now was in the hands of the Feds. They'd completely sealed off the farmhouse and had removed everything from the secret room. It was all now being processed by specialists and high tech computer programs to see if any of it could shed any light on where Flint had gone. For now, though, Finn had a bit of spare time and he intended to put it to good use.

Switching on the garage light, the mere sight of the car calmed him. He had put it off long enough; he needed to confront the issue with Kat and get his head around it once and for all; working on the car always helped him focus.

Over the years he'd imagined all kinds of reasons why Kat had left town all those years ago and yet he'd never considered that she might be pregnant. He'd thought that what they'd had had been good enough that she would have told him about something like that.

Sitting on that hill months ago after she'd returned, he hadn't been prepared for the news that he had a son. She'd tried to explain, to tell him that she'd done it for his own good, but he hadn't been able to get past the fact that she'd had a son; his son, and she'd kept it from him all these years.

At first he'd been angry. Who did she think she was to make a decision like that without telling him? To give his son away to strangers without telling him? Those questions still remained but the anger had faded, giving way to an understanding of sorts. He wasn't sure he would ever entirely be able to get past it, but he knew now he wanted to try. They'd been good together, and nearly had been again, so it would be a shame now to lose that friendship without trying to save it.

Thirty-Six

He wasn't expecting to find Callahan in his office when he arrived the next morning but he was there, casually sitting behind Finn's desk.

"Do you mind? I think you'll find that's my desk." Finn waited for him to stand up and step out of the way before sitting down. "What are you doing here, anyway?"

"Well, I have some news and I thought you'd like to know about." He paused as if waiting for Finn to ask him what it was. *You'll have a long wait before I give you that satisfaction,* Finn thought.

Obviously giving up on getting a response, Callahan continued. "It looks like we may have a lead on Flint's whereabouts."

That got Finn's attention. "Where?"

"On our doorstep, just an hour's drive away. Our tech guys managed to identify quite a few of the faces on the videos using facial recognition software. Clever stuff. Anyway, comparing those names to a list of the numbers we got from his cell phone provider we found that he'd called one in particular several times on the day he locked Kat and Daniel in that dungeon." He was smiling now. "I've just had a call from our local office out there and they're about to carry out a raid on the premises."

"That's fantastic news. You didn't have to drive all the way over here to tell me that, though. You could have just called."

"I know, but I wanted to see if you wanted to tag along. They're waiting for me to give the word."

Finn was thrown. *Maybe you're not as bad as I thought you were.* "That's really good of you and yes, I do want to."

"Then let's go. We'll take my car."

Not arguing, Finn followed him downstairs and they set off, the tires screeching and the back end of the car sliding out as they left the station lot. "Try not to kill us before we get there, would you?" he muttered.

"Was there anything else recovered from the house?" Finn asked through clenched teeth as he hung on to the strap dangling from the ceiling for dear life.

"That safe under the rug? Well, it was filled with paperwork. It looks like Flint kept a record of all the dates and places when his men snatched a kid. We're not sure why, but possibly to keep from hitting the same place twice."

"At least that should make it easier to reunite any kids you do find with their families. How many were there?"

Callahan sighed. "Unbelievably, over fifty. We've managed to match all the dates and places with reported child disappearances but there was one thing that stood out. They were all boys except for one girl, one of the earlier victims."

"Why on earth would he take a girl? If he was using all his victims in this 'fight club', he would just want boys. It makes no sense."

"Agreed. Just one of the many things we'll be asking him when we get our hands on him."

***

What should have been an hour's drive in fact only took them forty-five minutes and Finn was certain that Callahan hadn't lifted his foot of the pedal once that whole time. The place they were headed was another innocuous looking farm that you wouldn't look twice at if you were driving past, never suspecting what was happening there.

About a mile away from their intended target, Callahan turned his car off the tarmacked road and onto a dirt side road. About half a mile down, he reached a parking area which was already full of emergency vehicles. There were several police cruisers, three ambulances and, of course, the FBI teams.

"Looks like you've got it well covered." Finn was impressed.

"We're not taking any chances. He's not getting away this time."

Finn went to open the car door but before he could he felt Callahan's hand on his arm. "You're here as an observer only, okay?" Finn nodded. He knew this was an FBI operation; he was just glad that he was going to be there to see the bastard taken into custody.

"Don't worry, I'm not going to do anything that'll jeopardize this bastard getting what's coming to him."

***

The plan was simple. The SWAT teams would surround the main farmhouse and the two barns stood nearby and, on a pre-arranged signal, would enter the building simultaneously taking anyone they found into custody. Everyone was aware that there were likely to be children present and that they didn't know where, so their instructions were clear: go in hard and fast but don't shoot unless you have to.

Finn and Callahan and all other non-SWAT personnel would remain at the rendezvous point and listen to the take-down over the radio. Once it was clear, they would then be called in.

"You got a spare pair of those?" Finn asked eyeing the binoculars that Callahan held up to his eyes.

"Over there, in the back of the van." Callahan indicated one of the FBI vans parked nearby.

Grabbing a pair, Finn took up position next to Callahan and together they watched in silence as the SWAT team moved in. The atmosphere was tense and there was no chatter at the RV point, everyone listening intently to the radio which was eerily silent.

The sudden burst of noise made Finn jump. They were in. For the next few minutes, it seemed that the radio was full of shouting and screaming, with SWAT screaming at people to get on the ground and put down their weapons, but thankfully there were no sounds of gunfire. Just as suddenly as it had erupted, the noise suddenly stopped.

"All clear, premises secure. All threats in custody," the SWAT team commander announced.

"Let's go." Callahan was already making his way to his car and Finn quickly followed, jumping into the passenger seat as the car started to move and barely having time to close the door before they left the dirt road and hit the tarmac, closely followed by the police cruisers and paramedics who had been waiting with them for the all clear.

As they pulled up to the farmhouse, the SWAT team was just leading their prisoners out of the house in handcuffs. Finn immediately recognized one of them as being the man they'd seen on the CCTV footage but there was no sign of Flint.

"Are there any more in there?" he asked the SWAT commander, who was bringing up the rear holding his own prisoner.

"No, this is all of them."

He had to be there! "There's one missing. He's got to be here."

"We've cleared the premises. There's no one else in there."

Turning away, he saw that the farm hand was about to be loaded into the back of a prison van. Running over to him, he grabbed him by his shirt front and would have pulled him off his feet if he had hadn't been held up by the officer holding him. "Where is he? Where's Flint?" he yelled in his face.

"No comment," he answered, smirking.

Finn hadn't realized he'd pulled his arm back, prepared to take a punch, until he felt a hand on his arm. "I don't think you want to do that." Callahan pulled him away.

"Flint's not here."

"I know, but we'll find him. It's over for them now. There's nowhere for him to hide. It's only a matter of time before we track down everyone who took part in this operation. We'll get him."

"You're right." Finn took a deep breath, steadying himself. "I'll go and check the barns, see if they've found any of the kids yet."

They'd assumed that it would be likely that the set-up here would be similar to the set up at the Flint farm, so those waiting at the RV point had been told that their first priority was to check the barns. It had paid off. As Finn entered the first barn he could see that a trap door had been found and, as he watched, the first child was helped out of the depths and into the arms of a waiting paramedic.

His intense relief that they had found the kids was tinged with horror. *How many more places were there like this? How many more kids?* There was nothing he could do there; they had everything in hand. The barn, the yard, everywhere he looked was a hive of activity with people milling about, talking into radios.

About five hundred yards from the back of the barn he could see a small outbuilding, no more than a hut really, that no one seemed to be paying any attention to. The hut was small, no more than five yards wide and a couple of yards tall. It seemed like a fairly new structure, the wood still being in good condition with no sign of rot, but Finn struggled to understand what it could be used for. It was too small for farm animals or machinery, so something about it struck him as strange.

"Hey!" he called out to one of the SWAT team waiting to load his prisoner into the back of the van. "Anyone check that hut out?"

His prisoner picked that moment to try and head-butt him. Stepping out of the way, he shouted back, "Everything's been cleared," before taking his prisoner to the ground.

Finn decided to check it out for himself. The noise from the activity taking place at the farmhouse dimmed as he moved further away and closer to the hut, until eventually he could hardly hear it at all. Walking around the outside, he couldn't find any windows and there was only one door. A padlock hung from it, but it was open and unlocked.

Finn was curious but had no sense of danger as he opened the door. He'd barely put one foot inside before he was stopped in his tracks.

"One more move and I'm putting a bullet in your brain."

The voice came from his right. Looking out of the corner of his eye, he saw Flint step from the shadows holding a gun pointed directly at his head.

"Raise your hands."

Finn did as he was told, his mind racing. *The building was supposed to be clear!*

"Now step inside." He stood stock still, barely breathing as Flint moved behind him and closed the door before coming to stand in front of him.

"Hello, Finn. I wish I could say it was nice to see you but under the circumstances, I'd be lying."

"You know there's no way out, don't you?"

He nodded. "Yes, it would seem that way. But there's no reason why I can't take a couple of you with me."

"What is this place?" Finn looked around, trying to distract him.

"This? Ah well, this is where my colleague sends his boys when they've been very naughty. He sometimes forgets they're out here, unfortunately. He's lost a couple that way." He chuckled

Finn felt sick. "So what's your plan? They're going to notice I'm not around very soon and come looking for me."

"And they'll find you. They'll just be too late to save you."

Everything seemed magnified in that moment as Finn watched Flint's finger start to squeeze the trigger. Everything else in the room lost focus and all he could see was the trigger start to move under the pressure.

In that millisecond, he had time to be surprised that his life wasn't flashing before his eyes. Wasn't that what was supposed to happen?

"Get down!" The shout took him by surprise, but he instantly dropped to his knees as the door behind him flung open at the same time a shot was fired. He watched as Flint was knocked off his feet by a shot to the shoulder, crying out in pain as the impact sent him twisting as he fell, his gun flying out of his hand.

"I thought I told you, you were here as an observer only?"

Finn got to his feet as Callahan retrieved Flint's gun from the floor.

"What took you so long?" Finn took his cuffs from his belt and secured Flint's hands as Callahan called for someone to come and take him into custody.

"You'll never get us all. We're everywhere," Flint panted as he lay on the floor, bleeding.

"Make sure you tell that to your cellmate," Finn tossed over his shoulder as he walked out the door. "I'm sure he'll enjoy trying to wipe you all out, starting with you."

***

"How did you know I was in there?" Finn asked as they made their way back to the main farmhouse behind them.

"I heard you ask about the hut. I did shout and tell you to wait but you didn't hear me, I guess. When I saw the door close it seemed odd. Why would you need to close the door? So I thought I'd check it out."

"Well I'm glad you did, but how on earth did you know he had a gun to my head?"

"I heard the voices when I got close and there was a small hole in the wall, just big enough for me to be able to figure out what was going on."

"Well, thank you. It would seem I owe you one." Finn shook his hand. "Maybe you're not as bad as I thought you were after all."

"Just don't hug me, okay?"

Laughing, Finn agreed. "So where are you taking them?"

"To the local jail for now. I'm going to interview Flint as soon as he's had medical treatment. We can't afford to waste any time."

"Can I sit in?"

"How did I know you were going to ask that? You can observe. Best I can do."

"Good enough."

Thirty-Seven

Finn looked at his old high school teacher through the glass. Though physically it was clearly the same man, he seemed different. Whether it was the fact that Finn now knew what terrible secrets he had hidden, or whether it was because now that he was in custody he'd let his mask slip, he didn't know.

"His lawyer's here at last, now we can get started." Callahan had been pacing back and forth for the last two hours waiting for him to arrive. Flint had refused to say anything and had immediately lawyered up when they'd started to question him.

Finn watched as Callahan made his way into the room and sat down across the table from them.

"Mr Flint, you know what you're here for. Do yourself a favor and tell us everything you know. We know there are a lot more of you, if you co-operate I'll tell the judge and who knows, he might go easier on you."

Flint smirked. "No comment."

Callahan carried on "you know, these are very serious charges and we're in a death penalty state. Your cooperation could be the difference between life in prison or the needle."

Flint leaned over to talk to his lawyer before sitting back in his chair and crossing his arms. "Get the D.A. down here and if the deal is good enough, I may be able to help you."

Suspending the interview, Callahan left the room. "Bastard lawyer" he spat as he joined Finn in the viewing room. "We need that information so I'll have to speak to the D.A. and see what they can do.

They spent another restless hour drinking bad coffee from the machine in the corridor waiting for the D.A. to arrive, and it took another two hours to come to a deal that Flint and his lawyer were happy with. Finn wasn't happy about it, though. He wanted to see the bastard die for what he'd done, but if they wanted to know about the others involved and what had happened to the other kids, they'd had to agree to take the death penalty off the table.

Eventually, though, he started talking and what he told them was worse than anything they'd imagined.

The network of fight clubs was at least fifty strong, and all of them were holding young boys captive. He seemed to get a thrill out of telling them that it spanned the whole of the United States and had been in operation for decades. He'd told them about his black book containing details of all the clubs and it was immediately retrieved from his property. A massive operation would be mounted by the FBI in the coming days to raid all of the premises listed simultaneously.

Thankfully, Flint's pride had stopped him alerting the others to his failure.

The most shocking revelation though came when he was asked what had happened to all the kids he had kidnapped over the years that were no longer kept in his dungeon. He showed no emotion, no remorse, as he calmly told them that the ones that didn't make it, or who weren't considered good enough, were buried in one of the fields on his farm. Shockingly, he couldn't remember the exact number; they meant that little to him.

Thirty-Eight

The weather suited the mood as they stood in the field two days later. The sky was gray and the rain had started again, soaking the ground and making puddles in the mud. "Why don't you go home? I'll call you with any news."

Kat could see the concern on Finn's face but she had no intention of leaving. "No, I'm staying." She was pleased he didn't argue. She didn't want to have to explain that she felt she needed to be here in this terrible place. Needed to be here for the boys. She'd left Daniel at home with Jamie; he was safe now but these boys, they had no one here to care for them so it felt right that she be here.

Callahan had organized the activity now taking place in the field. There was a team who specialized in body recovery, a team of forensic anthropologists and several senior FBI officials. It was left to them now, and all they could do was watch and wait.

"I am sorry, you know," she said. "Sorrier than you'll ever know." She turned to look at him but he kept facing the field.

"I know."

"Are we ever going to be able to move past this?" She needed to know. She'd waited long enough and after everything she'd been through over the past few days she didn't want to wait any longer.

He turned to her then. "It hurt, Kat. Not just what you did. I can understand that, I guess, though it would have been different if you'd just told me. No, what hurt the most was that for twenty years you stayed away and kept this from me." He sighed "If you hadn't come back for Jamie, would you ever have told me?"

"Probably not." She knew she had to honest with him if she wanted any chance of salvaging any part of their relationship.

He nodded, as if she was confirming something he already knew. "But I've learned over the past few days just how fleeting life is. So yes, Kat, we'll get past this. It just may take a little time."

She couldn't ask for anything more, so left it there and turned her attention back to the field.

***

It didn't take long for the first body to be found and over the next few days, the whole field was probed until they were happy that they'd recovered all the bodies that had been buried there. It would take months to identify the remains and return them to their families, but at least they would be going home at last.

"Coffee?" Finn asked, pouring out two cups.

"Sure, that would be good." Callahan took the offering and led the way into the chief's office.

"So today was the last day out on the field?"

"Yep. All the kids on the list are accounted for except one. The forensic anthropologist was able to tell us that, although they've not been identified yet, none of the bodies recovered was female."

"So what happens now?"

"Well, we've tried to question Flint some more but as soon as we mentioned the girl he clammed up. We won't be getting any more out of him. We're going to have to face the possibility that we'll never find out what happened to her."

Thirty-Nine

"Okay, we're off!" Jamie's voice reached her in the kitchen.

"Hang on!" Wiping her hands, which were wet from washing the breakfast dishes, she quickly went into the hall. Daniel, holding Jamie's hand, was beaming, clearly excited.

"So you got everything?" She counted the items off on her hand. "Sunscreen, hat, pocket money?"

"Yeesssss! Can we go now?"

Kat laughed as she dropped to her knees and gave him a hug. "Sure, honey. Have a great time and be good for Jamie, okay?" She was taking him to a fair that was taking place in the next town over. Kat had wanted to take him, but it was her turn to visit Jake so Jamie had insisted on ditching work and taking him herself.

"Any problems call me, okay?" She directed this at Jamie.

"There won't be any. Give Jake my love."

Kat stood at the door, watching as they got in the car and then drove off, leaving her alone for the first time in days. She had an hour before she had to leave to make visiting time at the prison and she had a lot of stuff to catch up on. She hadn't been into the office for days and she still had all the property records that she'd borrowed from the town council office. If she was quick, she could drop the files back into town and come back via the office and check in.

Humming to herself, she went into the office at the back of the house to collect the files that she'd left there before all hell had broken loose. She hadn't even had chance to go through them and she clearly didn't need to now but curiosity, or just plain nosiness, got the best of her. Sitting down in the chair behind the desk, she went through the pile until she found the records for the farmhouse where she had been held. *That's odd.* The farmhouse wasn't in Flint's name; it was in the name of a Jayne Flint. Changing her plans, she decided that she would hang on to the records for another day and have a closer look tonight when she got back from the visit.

Her thoughts turned to her nephew as she set off on the drive to the prison. She hadn't really had any time to worry about what he'd said to Jamie over the past few days but now that she was on her way to see him, her initial concern returned and she was determined to find out what he meant.

Sitting at the same screen where Jamie had sat the week previously, Kat was shocked when Jake finally came through the door on the other side. One of his arms was in a sling and was quite obviously causing him pain from the way he cradled it. But what was even more shocking was his face. As he sat down opposite her, Kat took in the swollen and bruised left eye socket and cheek and the nasty cut to his lip. "What on earth happened?" she asked him as soon as he picked up the handset.

He wouldn't meet her eyes. "Something and nothing. No big deal."

"Are you kidding me? Have you looked in a mirror today?"

"Honestly, Kat, it's nothing. Please, don't push."

She could hear the tone in his voice and it worried her. He really didn't want her to push this, but why? "Jake, what's going on?" She kept her voice low. "What you said to your sister, about if anything happens to you, what did you mean?"

He looked up and met her eyes then and there was no disguising the fear in them. "Nothing. I meant nothing, Kat. Please just leave it." She watched as he glanced at the guard before turning back to her. "I've got to go. I'm sorry," he said before quickly, hanging up the phone before she had the chance to reply and telling the guard he wanted to be taken back to his cell.

Stunned, Kat just sat there for a moment before standing up and making her way outside. *What was that all about?*

Forty

"Did you have a good time?" Kat asked as Daniel came barreling in and threw his arms around her neck. The change in him was incredible. As soon as he'd been told that Flint was in jail, it had been as if a switch had been flipped inside him and he felt safe enough to be a kid again.

"It was the best! Look what I got!"

Kat acted suitably impressed by the goldfish in a bag that he was holding out for her inspection. "Well, you'd better go to the kitchen and see if you can't find a bowl to put him in, then." She smiled as she watched him go, talking to the fish.

"He's a great kid, Kat, truly a great kid," Jamie said, also watching him go.

Once Kat was happy he was out of earshot, she turned to her. "You were right. Something's going on with Jake."

"I knew it. Did he say anything else today?"

"No, but something's obviously happened." She filled her in on what she'd seen.

"So, what do we do?"

"I'm going to talk to Finn and see what he suggests. Something is telling me that I shouldn't talk to the prison directly, but I don't know how else to approach this."

She had another reason to talk to Finn. Something was bothering her. It was probably nothing, but she had the feeling they were missing something.

"I'll go and talk to him tomorrow. I've got to head into town in the morning anyway, so I may as well pop in while I'm there."

The conversation ended there as Daniel returned with the goldfish, the bag and a small desert bowl. "Will this one be okay?"

Looking at each other Kat and Jamie both laughed. "I think he might need a bit more room than that. Come on, we'll help you look.

Forty-One

Leaving Daniel at home with Jamie, Kat put the land records in the back seat of her car and headed into town.

After dropping the files off and thanking the property records clerk, she walked to the police station where Sandy told her to go in to the squad room. She could see Finn sitting behind the chief's old desk in the office, talking to Callahan, and made her way over.

"Hi, sorry to interrupt," she said as she knocked on the open door.

Finn waved her in. "You didn't. We were just going over some last stuff about the case. Tying up a few loose ends."

"Well, that's one of the things that I wanted to see you about. I don't know how I'd forgotten it before, but something happened when I was held at the farmhouse."

"What, Kat?"

"Well, at one point he had me upstairs, trying to find out information about the investigation."

"Yep, you told us that."

"Yes, but what I forgot to tell you was that while I was there he took a phone call and from what I could tell at my end someone was giving him information on what the police were doing."

She watched as they exchanged a look. "What? What's going on?"

"Well, we figured he was getting his information from somewhere because that's the only way he could possibly have known we were coming and have gotten out of there so fast."

"Do you know where he was getting it from?"

Callahan shook his head. "No, that's the bit where we're stumped."

"He won't tell us," Finn chimed in, "and whoever it was was using an untraceable cell phone so we can't get it from his phone records.

"Well, maybe this will help. I looked at the land records before I took them back and there was a woman's name listed on the title."

"Really? Can you remember what it was, Kat?" Finn sat up straighter in his chair.

"Jayne Flint."

"What? I didn't think he had any family? He's never been married that I know of and he doesn't have any kids." Finn looked confused.

"I don't know but maybe he does have family that we just don't know about?"

"Well, it's certainly something we need to look into. Thanks, Kat. I'm not sure how we missed this."

"You didn't. You had no way of knowing." She cleared her throat. "Anyway, that's not why I came to see you. I wanted to talk to you about Jake."

"Would you like me to give you some privacy?" Callahan asked, preparing to stand.

"No, not at all." Kat reassured him.

"How's he coping?" Finn had known Jake all his life and although they hadn't been close, they'd been friends.

"Not well." Kat told him about Jamie's visit and then her own. "Something's going on but he won't tell us what." She paused. "I think it has something to do with one of the guards but I'm not sure, that's why I don't want to go to the prison directly."

"Do you want me to go and talk to him?" Finn offered.

"Yes, please, Finn. Thank you, that would be great. Are you sure you don't' mind?"

"Not at all. Once this case is all wrapped up, I'll get it organized."

"Great! Okay, I'd better head back." Feeling happier about the Jake situation, Kat left. She was looking forward to spending a peaceful afternoon at home with Jamie and Daniel now that this was all over. For them at least.

Forty-One

"Thank you for meeting me." Kat closed the door to the doctor's office behind her. It seemed strange being back here. This is where it had all started what seemed like such a long time ago now.

"No problem. You said it was about Daniel?" Sally led Kat into her consulting room and made herself comfortable behind her desk. "How's he doing?"

"Well, that's what I wanted to talk to you about. He can't seem to stop having nightmares and I was hoping you'd be able to give me something that would help him sleep. He really needs the rest. He's nowhere near well yet."

"Shouldn't you be talking to his therapist about this? It's more an issue of dealing with what's causing the nightmares than trying to resolve the symptoms with drugs."

"You're probably right. I just thought I'd ask as he hasn't got another appointment with her for a week."

"Have you tried talking through what's causing the nightmares with him?"

Kat sighed. "Yes, it's usually the same thing. He dreams about this girl that was with him in that place, Jayne. They haven't been able to find her body and he dreams about her being alone out there somewhere. It's quite awful for him."

"Yes, I'm sure it must be. Well, as I said, it's really a matter for his therapist so I'm afraid I really can't help." She stood up and came around the desk and opened the door. "I really must get going. It's late already and I've got an early shift at the hospital tomorrow."

Kat stood to leave. "Okay. Thanks, Jayne."

"No problem," she replied before immediately realizing her mistake. Her face quickly became hard. "Very clever, Kat." She closed the door again.

Kat watched as she carefully walked back to her desk, sitting down once more. "It is you, isn't it?"

"You seem to have it all figured out. Why don't you tell me?"

"Jayne Flint, daughter of Mark Flint. You're the one who made the phone calls tipping him off, aren't you?"

Jayne clapped. "Well done, Kat. How did you figure it out?"

"She didn't, I did."

Kat watched Jayne's eyes open wide as the door to the office swung open.

"How?"

"I didn't want to think it," Finn answered, "and I'm not sure what triggered the suspicion, but every time I asked you about your background you got very cagey."

"What? That's it? Just because a girl doesn't tell you her life story doesn't mean she's hiding anything, Finn."

Finn nodded. "No, you're right. But I asked you about whether you had any family here and it seemed to hit a nerve." He shrugged. "Far-fetched, I know, but I had to follow my hunch. So I reached out to the hospital who gave me your personnel file. That, in turn, led me to your medical school."

Jayne had gone pale now as she listened to him. "They had no record of a Sally Crichton having ever attended there, but a Jayne Flint did."

Kat watched as Finn read her rights and handcuffed her before turning to look at her. "Thanks, Kat. We needed to hear her admit it but if I'd have done it, any good defense attorney would have got it excluded at trial because of my relationship with her."

Kat just nodded before turning to Jayne. "How could you do it? How could you help him get away with everything he did to those kids?"

"He's my father. He raised me single-handedly. He sent me to the best boarding schools, paid my college tuition and for medical school. He's the only family I've got and I owe him. What choice did I have?"

Kat felt sad as she watched Finn take her away. She could have stopped him, could have saved all those children, but instead she chose to help him.

Forty-Three

Neither of them spoke as they sat on the deck. It was over at last. "You want another?" Finn asked raising his beer bottle

"No, I'm good, thanks." Kat smiled. She'd missed this.

"So how's Daniel doing?"

She beamed; he was her favorite subject. "He's doing great. The therapist is really happy with his progress. And, I've got an announcement to make."

"Oh, yeah? What's that?"

"I'm going to adopt him, if they'll let me."

"Really? That's fantastic news." Finn seemed genuinely pleased. She'd been a bit worried about telling him, not knowing how he would take it seeing as she'd given up their son for adoption but his reaction told her she'd worried about nothing.

The chime of the doorbell interrupted them and Kat sipped happily at her beer while Finn went to answer it. He returned quickly with Callahan in tow.

"Beer?" Finn offered.

"Yes, please."

Finn disappeared into the kitchen, returning with a bottle for Callahan and another one for himself.

"How did the raids go?" Kat knew they'd been due to take place earlier that day.

"Fantastic, exactly as planned. All of the clubs are now out of action and we've recovered hundreds of kids."

"That's great news. I'll sleep better knowing those bastards have been put away," Kat said with feeling. "It's strange, you know. Jayne was the same age as we are and I don't remember her from high school."

"I might be able to shed a bit of light on that." Callahan took a sip of his beer. "We couldn't find any birth records for her so I told them to dig deeper." He reached into his back pocket and took out two sheets of paper, one for each of them. "This is what they found."

The sheets were copies of a missing person flyer from thirty years ago. On it was the picture of a young girl, no more than about eight years old. Her name was Rita. "From what we've learned, it seems that Rita was a bit of a tomboy. Dressed like a boy, acted like a boy. She was cycling to a friend's house and just vanished."

Kat was confused. "Sorry, you've lost me."

"It's her isn't it?" Finn spoke up and Callahan nodded.

"Yes, it is. We think that she was taken because she looked so much like a boy. A mistake. We're going to try and get confirmation from Flint if he'll talk to us, but it looks like he decided to raise her as his own."

The enormity of what he was saying hit home and Kat felt sick. Despite what Jayne had done, she had ultimately been just another victim. "Has her family been told?"

"It's in process." Callahan sighed. "That's not a visit I would want to make."

They all sat in silence for a minute, taking it all in.

"I think I'll have that beer after all." Kat stood up and went inside to grab one.

Closing the fridge door, she jumped. "You scared me!"

Callahan stood there grinning at her. "Sorry, didn't mean to make you jump!" he said, not looking at all sorry. "I just wanted to ask, now that this is all over, if you'd like to have dinner with me sometime?"

Taken aback, she wasn't sure what to say. Things were on a better footing now with Finn but she didn't think they were ever going to get back together. He'd given her no indication that that was something he was even considering. And here was a handsome, smart man asking her out. "Yes," she said, making up her mind. "Yes, I'd like that very much."

Neither of them noticed Finn by the door and he turned and went back outside before they did.

Forty-Four

Pick up, pick up! He'd been trying Kat's cell for the last ten minutes but it just rang before switching to voicemail. Shivering, Jake wrapped his arms around his middle to try and warm himself up. *At least it's not raining!*

He'd walked miles before coming across this gas station with what was probably the only working payphone round these parts. Unfortunately, it was out in the open so he ducked back into the trees that lined the rear of the property after trying her phone one more time. At least they provided some protection from the prying eyes of the nearby road. But he couldn't stay here long, he had to keep moving.

He'd had no choice; he wouldn't have made it out alive if he'd stayed in that place any longer; they would have made sure of that. A tragic accident, or killed by another prisoner maybe, but somehow they would make sure he didn't talk.

He would stay here for another half an hour and then he would have to move on. He'd considered calling Jamie when he couldn't get hold of Kat but had quickly dismissed the idea. After everything he had put her through, he wasn't dragging her into this now. No, he needed to get hold of Kat. She was the only one who could help him now.

The End

If you have any comments, please contact me via my Facebook page. Thank you!

www.facebook.com/ajcarella
www.twitter.com/@ajcarella

7670905R00104

Printed in Great Britain
by Amazon.co.uk, Ltd.,
Marston Gate.